The Falcon's Final Flight

By:

Ivan Wikert

Acknowledgments

I would like to thank my wife, Ronna for her many long hours of editing, and her unwavering confidence and support for my writing.

This book's cover is courtesy of PublicDomainPictures.net

Chapter 1

The midnight hour had passed, the sea had calmed, and the island city of Tyre was fast asleep. Darkness had finally taken hold on the hills along the coastline that looked out over the Mediterranean Sea. Moving quietly through the water was a man dressed in a dark blue wet suit, fins, and a mask. His name was David Stone. He was a twenty-five year old American from Southern California, and a United States Navy Seal. He had walked into the Mediterranean six hours earlier just north of the town of Betzet on Israel's deserted northern shore. It would not be long now before he walked out of the water, and into the territory of the enemy. The three months of planning and intense training in a small obscure facility, not a stone's throw from the town of Netanya in the state of Israel, would be put to the test on this very night.

The young Seal's target was a dangerous and elusive terrorist with close ties to Hezbollah. His code name was Falcon, and for more than a decade, he had been at the top of Israel's Most Wanted List.

David's dark green fins continued to move up and down methodically below the surface, propelling his six foot, one hundred eighty pound frame quietly along through the darkness. The only signs of life he had seen since leaving Israel were a few ships and fishing boats along the coastline.

On the shore, date palms lined the sparsely lit pathway above where the white sand joined with the incoming tide as it gently washed ashore. The island city of Tyre jutted out from the coast into the Mediterranean, twenty-five kilometers north of the Israeli border. Before 334 B.C., when Alexander the Great constructed a causeway from the mainland, the city of Tyre was an island unto itself, but the storms of centuries past had pushed up sand from the depths to settle against Alexander's ancient stone bridge. Tyre was now just another Lebanese city along the Mediterranean Coast.

As David swam across the opening of the quiet cove, he could hear the rippling sea slapping against the rocky outcropping ahead. For the first time in over six long, grueling hours, his feet touched solid ground. He felt the huge stones from centuries of crumbling civilizations beneath his feet, and he could smell the plankton and sea life that had adhered itself to the sea wall. He slid slowly over and then up onto one of the huge slimy stones and sat up, looking back over the blackish surface of the Mediterranean. It seemed almost fitting that, nestled in a sea of stars high overhead, there was a crescent moon. It was much larger and brighter, but closely resembled the one on the flags that flew over most of the Middle Eastern countries. There were no guards patrolling along the seawall, no fishermen in the harbor, and no one between him and the buildings at the end of the long, concrete-capped wall.

According to Israeli Intelligence, a large white three-story building made of stone imported from Italy's distant shore would be sitting at the end of the seawall, overlooking the harbor and the Mediterranean. It was a four-star hotel at a time when Tyre was considered to be the playground of the rich in the Middle East. After many years of war and uncertainty, the Grand Hotel no longer catered to tourists. Instead, it was now home to Hezbollah leadership, and it was the last known whereabouts of Ahmed Ali Muhammad, AKA, The Falcon.

David sat down on the rocks and removed his mask and the hood that covered his short-cropped, dark brown hair. He rubbed his face, ran his hands through his hair, and then removed the specially designed waterproof bag attached to his belt before climbing to higher ground. He removed the fins from his feet and pulled the zipper that ran from end to end of the utility bag. Rolled up tight inside was a dark green long sleeved pullover and matching sweat pants. He removed his twenty-two-magnum automatic, designed by Israeli Intelligence, and a service belt. Next, he removed five, twenty-five-round clips of ammo, a service knife, and a pair of black sneakers.

After one more careful look around, he unzipped his wet suit, peeling the soft wet rubber from his well-conditioned body. He unrolled the sweatpants and pulled them on. Next, he slipped the pullover over his head, then the service belt, knife and firearm fell quickly into place. He filled the now-empty utility bag with his wet suit, fins, and mask, zipped it, and pushed it into a void between two large stones. He stood up, slipped his bare feet into his shoes, and took one more look around.

From where he had come ashore, he could see the high rises marking the skyline off in the distance, and he could hear the waves breaking gently along the shoreline at his feet. He moved up onto the surface of the deserted jetty and began the long walk to the hotel.

The Israeli's were right; the building was just where they said it would be. He was now just twenty yards away, and all that stood between him and the old three story hotel was one dark, dimly lit street. Twin date palms, with their fronds dancing on the gentle sea breeze, marked the entrance to the hotel. Above the massive arched doorway, a single light shone down from the roof, shedding light on a once-ornate plaza and fountain in front of an otherwise dark and foreboding structure. All the elongated windows but one were void of light all along the front and seaward side of the building, the one exception being on the third floor in the front, just above and right of the front door.

There were six vehicles parked to the left of the entrance facing the seawall. One was a far-from-new, black Mercedes Sedan and the other five were newer four-wheel drive Land Rovers.

David's brown eyes scanned for movement up and down the roadway as he quickly made his way across the empty street, stopping in the shadow of the swaying palms.

He removed his weapon from his side without looking down, quickly opening and releasing the slide. The silencer was already in place on the business end of the automatic and, with the touch of his right forefinger, he activated the laser sight. He stood up slowly and took one more look around to make sure the coast was clear before moving quickly through the Plaza.

He had the building's floor plan engraved in his memory and, as he covered the last twenty feet to the door, he perused the blueprints in his mind. He knew that it would be dark inside the building, and his success or failure, and most assuredly his life, depended on an unseen familiarity to his surroundings. His shadow stretched out on the patterned marble floor and then disappeared suddenly when he closed the thick wooden door behind him.

He moved along the dining room wall, counting his steps while avoiding the tables and chairs along the way. He kept his left hand on the wall, a firm grip on his weapon and, with his right hand, he searched in the darkness for the door leading into the stairwell.

So far so good. Everything is just as it was supposed to be, he thought to himself when he found the door. When he opened it, he found the stairwell illuminated by one small, flickering light bulb at the head of each of the three landings. It was quiet when he ascended the first thirteen marble steps to the landing on the second floor. There, he paused just long enough to listen and scan the next flight of stairs, and then moved up quickly to the third and final landing.

The grab handle made a clicking sound as he took hold of it and then the solid metal door opened into a hallway. There were six rooms to his left and the same number to his right. It was almost pitch black in the hallway after the door behind him closed, but as his eyes adjusted, he could see the elongated windows at each end of the long hallway.

According to Israeli Intelligence, Ahmed Ali Muhammad had moved his family to the city in July of 2006 during the last Israeli invasion and now, at the behest of Hezbollah, occupied the entire third floor of the hotel. They had gleaned this information through one of his younger children's schoolteachers who was a Mossad Agent. On that information alone, the plan to assassinate the Falcon was born. What they did not know was in which of the twelve rooms David would find Ahmed at 1:45 am.

He turned to his right and moved slowly down the dimly lit hallway, stopping briefly to listen in front of each door. The doorknob on the room at the far end of the hallway turned easily and he silently entered the room. The small red dot that would lead the small caliber round to its mark scanned the room for a target but found none.

The faint light from the moon, which filtered in through the windows, showed him that there were two single beds on each side of the window. And with the exception of a single folded blanket and small pillow, the mattresses were bare. A round table and two chairs filled the space to his right. On the left side of the room, there were two doors; the one leading to the bathroom was closed, but the one that connected to the empty room next door, was slightly ajar.

David crossed the twelve-foot wide room and opened one door and then the other. As he entered the adjoining room, he saw that the two beds in the room were occupied, and leaning against the window between the bunks were two assault rifles. He moved in closer until he was between the beds, made sure his targets were grown men and not boys, and then fired two quick shots. The silenced twenty-two made little noise, and each of his sleeping targets flinched and then became motionless. He removed the blanket from one and then the other, checking for a scar that he had been told marked his target's face. The two dead men wore full beards and looked to be in their thirties, but neither had the markings he was looking for.

He turned his attention to the doors leading to the next room. They were closed but unlocked, and when he pushed the last remaining barrier inward, a faint light greeted him. The source of the light came from inside the bathroom, and spread out to illuminate the room and four single beds, all of them occupied, but from the size of the four figures hidden under the covers, he knew that they had to be children. David moved on to the next set of doors, not wanting to even consider what he would have to do if one of those innocent kids opened their eyes.

The next set of doors was standing wide open, and his shadow preceded him through the opening. The light that followed him in from where the children slept also guided him to the foot of two more beds. Only one of the two was in use. He removed his finger from the trigger and touched the switch that brought the small red laser dot to bear, but quickly turned it off when he noticed he had pointed out a woman. It may have been the brief appearance of the laser, or maybe she just sensed something, but either way, she began to stir. He backed away quickly and moved through the next set of open doors just as the woman opened her eyes.

The room he found himself standing in was empty and dark, and the doors leading into the next room were closed. He moved quickly across the room, opened the door, then closed it behind himself just as the woman turned on the light in the one he had just vacated. He had been in four out of the six rooms on one side of the stairwell, and was standing in the middle of the fifth one.

Light was now streaming in from beneath the door in the next room, and he could see by the interruptions in the light's pattern that the woman was moving around inside. He backed away from the door until his back pressed against the next room's access, all the while keeping his weapon trained on the door.

"*Please do not open that door Lady. I don't want to have to kill you,*" he said to himself."

6

He reached behind his back, found the knob opening the first door, and fumbled for the next. The knob on the door he was facing turned and light began to filter in around the jam as it slowly opened inward. He brought his weapon up, leveled it on the door and tried to convince himself that he had no choice. But then for some reason, the door stopped its inward movement and the latch closed.

He was relieved, and slowly exhaled the deep breath he had been holding before pushing his way into the next room. He closed the door behind himself, moved across room number six to the door that led back out into the hallway, and turned on the light.

There were no beds in the room; just a small round table surrounded by a half dozen chairs. There was a frameless picture of Osama Bin Laden taped to the wall, and a plastic wrapped six-pack of Fiji water bottles on the floor underneath the table. On top of the table was a map of Egypt, and a week old copy of As-Safir. The headline had been circled in ink. It read, "EGYPT TO HOST Peace Talks," and someone had circled Cairo on the map in red ink.

He sat down in one of the chairs and extracted the six-pack of water from the floor. This was the first fresh water he had been close to in over six hours. He pushed the map to one side and turned his attention to the newspaper. According to the date, the paper was three days old, and the Peace Talks were scheduled for the fourteenth, just two days away. He folded the map and the Lebanese newspaper, and was just about to slip them into his waistband when he noticed a single piece of white paper slip from the pages and fall to the floor at his feet. He picked it up and immediately saw that there were only two Arabic symbols scribbled on the six by nine inch piece of paper and, translated to English, it spelled out Sea Eagle. He added the piece of paper to his collection, folded the map inside the newspaper and slipped them inside his shirt. He finished off the bottle of water and then got to his feet.

As he turned toward the door leading to the hallway, the door he had just come through opened. He found himself face to face with a woman. She was dressed all in white, and was holding her headscarf across her mouth with her left hand. She was less than five feet tall and was small boned, judging by her slender wrist and tiny fingers. She had a look of fear and anxiety in her dark brown eyes when she saw David standing there with his weapon trained on her.

She suddenly let the headscarf fall away from her face, and her expression quickly changed.

"Ahmed is not here," she said in Arabic while pushing the door closed behind her.

David lowered the twenty-two automatic, removing the red dot from her chest, and asked,

"Where is he?"

"He has gone to Egypt. He left last night."

"Who are you to the one they call the Falcon?"

"I am wife number three."

"Where are number one and number two?"

"They are across the hall."

Now David knew that this young woman could not be the mother of the four children in the other room. *Hell, she is just a kid herself,* he reasoned.

"How old are you?"

"I will be fifteen soon," she answered and then moved closer to David.

"Please Sir, I wish for you to kill me," she added.

She held out her small hand, touched the silencer on the end of David's automatic and lifted it up, directing the barrel to a spot at the center of her chest.

"I would prefer death to life with Ahmed."

"What is your name?"

"Badra."

"Where is your family?"

"They live in Sidon. It is to the north of here."

"Why don't you just walk out that door and

8

go home?"

"That is not possible, Sir. Ahmed paid my father. I have no place to go, so I beg you to kill me."

"Badra, I came here to kill Ahmed, not his fourteen year old slave. Are you sure he is on his way to Egypt?"

"Yes, they are planning to kill someone there."

"How do you know that he is going to Egypt?"

"Seleh told me."

"Who is Seleh?"

"Ahmed's oldest son."

"What do you know about the Sea Eagle?"

"It is a cargo ship. It was here in the harbor until last night."

"You saw the Sea Eagle in the harbor?"

"No, Sir. Seleh told me that they had booked passage on the ship."

"I see. Thank you for the information Badra. And I'm sorry I can't do what you ask, but I promise you that before you turn fifteen, you will be a widow." She smiled when she heard what he said, and removed her hand from the barrel of the twenty-two automatic.

The Falcon once again was one step ahead of justice. However, if Badra was right and the Falcon was en route to Cairo, they might have a second chance to take him out. All David had to do now was get back to Israel, find his contact, and either find the Sea Eagle or get to Cairo in three days.

He put his index finger to her lips and told her to keep quiet. She moved to the door, lifted her headscarf to cover her face, and opened it. She walked out into the hallway, looked both ways, and then motioned to David that the coast was clear. He moved quickly down the hallway and back into the stairwell. Badra stood in the hallway watching him as he slipped through the door.

He moved quickly down the stairs to the ground floor, and wasted no time exiting the building. It was three hundred yards back down to the seawall where he had stashed his gear, and he would need it if he was going to make the six-hour swim back to Israel's distant shore. But then he thought to himself, *why swim when there is a harbor full of boats?*

He followed a narrow cobblestone pathway through one of the stone archways to the first wooden-planked pier. The pontoon-supported pier was only four feet wide, and rocked back and forth under his weight as he made his way from boat to boat. There was more than an ample supply of small watercraft. Some of them newer speedboats, but most of them were old wooden-hulled Boston Whaler type fishing boats. Finding one with enough fuel on board for the journey back to Israel was another story.

He had been in and out of six different vessels before settling on an old fifteen-foot wooden hulled skiff with a single outboard motor. The tank that was hooked up to the engine seemed to be full enough, and under a bench near the back of the fifteen-foot bucket was a spare that appeared to be topped off. The thirty-five horsepower outboard came to life after three pulls, and the engine's sound permeated the sleeping harbor. He moved forward and cast off the bowline, then pushed the boat away from the pier. With the stolen craft's bow turned into the wind, he opened the throttle, leaving behind a phosphorous trail in the water, and sped away from the pier. The small boat's wake rolled out away from the bow, disturbing the mirror like surface of the harbor, and sending out a small wave to wash against the stone seawall.

Far off in the distance, a lighthouse's intermittent beam danced off the side of the rocks until he was beyond the breakwater. He turned the bow south into the incoming sea breeze on a course for Israel's coastline. The old boat was not fast, but it would get him where he needed to go.

Off the bow to the east, evidence of the sun's return was beginning to show on the horizon. Within the hour, the cover of darkness he now enjoyed would be gone, and there was fifteen miles of enemy-controlled water between

Ivan Wikert

him and the beach near Betzet.

The Mediterranean was asleep and lay quiet under the quarter moon when he slipped unseen into Tyre, but as the sun came up to greet the morning, the sea began to push gently up from the depths. The small outboard motor strained to find the top of the slow-rolling swells and then rested beyond the crest as it descended into the void.

The ball of fire rose up from behind the horizon and was in full view when David noticed a boat in the distance. It was still a long way off, but it looked to be coming straight at him, and it was moving fast. He pushed for what little power was left in the thirty-five horse motor, and then turned the bow away from the coastline. He knew that the old bucket was not going to outrun the larger boat, but he had to try.

The coastline of Lebanon was fading away, but the much larger powerboat had closed the distance to just a few hundred meters. It was now clear to David that the boat bearing down on him was a patrol boat, and the flag flying above her deck was not Israeli. He knew that if they were Lebanese they would most likely want to take him into custody, and that was not an option. He brought the throttle back to idle, and then cut the power. When the swells rose up between him and the oncoming patrol boat, he went over the side.

The Lebanese patrol boat's engines backed off, then reversed just before bumping into the small fishing boat. He felt the boat rock when someone jumped down into her from the patrol boat. He silently slipped below the surface.

"There is no one on board," he heard a man yell in Arabic just as he surfaced on the other side of the patrol boat.

"Look for contraband," the man behind the helm, yelled in reply.

"There is nothing here but fishing gear," he heard someone say.

David slipped along the port side of the boat toward

11

the bow. The Lebanese crew members were still to starboard with all eyes on the abandoned boat when he pulled himself up quietly onto the deck. He counted three men in uniform on deck, and one was still over the side. "Tie the boat off. We will tow it back," he heard the man closest to him say just as he slipped down through the forward hatch.

It was just a minute or two before the patrol boat's engines powered up and David felt the boat turn. He moved aft through the small cabin to the open hatch, put his back to the wall and peered out onto the deck. Two of the men were standing with their backs to him, and a third was moving toward the cabin. The fourth he figured was right above his head at the helm. He remained still and concealed behind the bulkhead until his first target stepped down into the cabin. The Lebanese soldier's eyes noticed David, but before his brain had time to react, the four-inch blade in David's right hand opened his airway. The man fell to the floor. His mouth was moving as he was trying to cry out, but the only sound he managed was a gurgle as he gasped in vain for air.

One down, three to go, he thought to himself as he watched the man on the floor expire.

He still could not see the man above him at the helm, but he had a clear picture of the two near the stern. Both wore sidearms, and they were holstered. They were just seven feet from the cabin door, and he knew that he could easily kill them both without leaving the confines of the cabin. That would leave just the one he could not see to contend with. He was just about to step out into the open and take the shot when he noticed a shadow on the deck.

The pilot was coming down from the bridge, and still had both of his hands on the ladder when David stepped up and out of the cabin. He fired two shots from the hip, hitting the boats' Captain in the upper body. The man screamed out in pain as he fell away from the ladder and collapsed. His scream startled the two young

Lebanese seamen, causing them to turn around quickly, and find themselves looking down the barrel of David's handgun. The man on David's left immediately raised his hands above his head, but the man to his right moved his hand down toward his holstered revolver.

David shook his head no, and said in Arabic, "Don't be a fool, Seaman!"

The young man froze and then slowly raised his hands above his head.

"I want you two to slowly remove your service belts by the buckles. Do it slowly and then throw them over the side. You first," David said, pointing to the man who had almost made a fatal mistake. One at a time, they unbuckled their belts and tossed them over the side.

David moved to the ladder, climbed quickly up onto the bridge and pulled the throttles back to neutral. The patrol boat slowed down and then came to rest on the rolling sea. He jumped back down onto the deck and said,

"Now, I want you to get into that fishing boat and go home."

The two soldiers did not hesitate. One pulled the small boat alongside, and they both quickly jumped from the deck of the patrol boat.

David climbed back up the ladder and pushed the throttles forward to bring the twin engines back to life. He turned the bow east and set the autopilot before returning to the deck. He had two passengers still on board and he did not want to take them with him to Israel. He lifted the Patrol Boat's Captain up off the deck and gave him the deep six. Then he did the same with the Seaman below deck.

Chapter 2

David could see the Israeli shoreline and the beach where his journey had started just a few hours earlier, but now he was faced with another problem, there was a large green Israeli Coast Guard vessel bearing down on him from the south. The fifty-five footer was well armed, and they had the Lebanese patrol boat in their sights.

"*Well hell, here we go again,*" he said, this time aloud, just before backing off on the power.

When the Israeli gunboat came alongside, David raised his arms above his head.

"By order of the Israeli Coast Guard, I want all hands on deck and all weapons discarded," an Officer with a bullhorn commanded. David slowly removed his weapon from his service belt, sliding it onto the seat as directed, and stepped back.

Six Israeli seamen, who were spread out on the deck above, trained their weapons down on him. Another crew member dropped a boarding ladder over the side when the patrol boat brushed alongside, and then two more armed seamen climbed down quickly into the bow.

"Leave your weapon there and come down," ordered an Ensign.

"I'm an American."

"Good for you. Like I said, leave your weapon and come down here." David complied with the order and the Ensign pointed to the ladder.

"After you."

David grabbed hold of the stainless steel rung and climbed quickly up onto the deck of the ship as he heard a voice behind him.

"There is no one else aboard, but there seems to be a lot of blood, Sir," the Seaman yelled up from the deck.

Ivan Wikert

The ship's Captain turned to his First Mate and said,
"Turn that patrol boat inside out, Aston."
Then he turned his attention to David and said,
"I am Captain Asher. Welcome to Israel."
"David Stone, Specialist, United States Navy."
"When did your Navy start using Lebanese Patrol
Boats?"
"They don't as a rule, but sometimes you have to
improvise."
"Do you have any identification on you, Specialist?"
"No, Captain, I went swimming last night from that
beach over there," he said pointing over the Captain's
shoulder.
The Captain looked over his shoulder toward where
David had pointed, then down at the Lebanese patrol boat
that the Ensign had now secured to the side of his ship.
With his attention on the patrol boat, he said,
"Can you explain to me how you came in
possession of that patrol boat?"
"It's a long story, Captain."
They were interrupted by the First Mate who had
just come back on board.
"Captain, there is no one else on board, but as I
initially reported, there is a lot of blood in the cabin and on
the deck. Oh, and I found this twenty-two-caliber
automatic on the bridge."
"That belongs to me," David said.
Captain Asher took the weapon from the First Mate,
and said,
"That will be all, Lieutenant."
He took one more long look at the patrol boat
before saying,
"Seaman, cut that Lebanese cutter loose. We don't
need to be the cause of another international incident."
"Yes, Sir."
David turned to the Captain, and said,
"Captain, if you could call Israeli Intelligence and
ask for Major Amnon, he will vouch for me."

15

The Falcon's Final Flight

Captain Asher turned to another one of his young sailors,

"Call Israeli Intelligence. Ask for Major Amnon, and patch the call through to the galley."

"Yes, Sir," the young sailor said before turning and double-timing it toward the bridge.

"Why don't you join me below deck while we wait, Specialist Stone? I will buy you a cold drink and you can try to explain this mess."

"Lead the way, Captain, and I wouldn't mind something to eat either."

He followed the Captain toward the stern and down the gangway to the galley. The two armed sentries the Captain had assigned to watch David closed the hatch and stood at rest at the bottom of the gangway.

Captain Asher opened one of two large reefer units and extracted two bottles of Israeli beer.

"Bottoms up, Specialist Stone. Isn't that what you Yanks always say?" David twisted the cap, releasing the aroma and a bit of foam and said,

"Cheers, Captain," as he hoisted the bottle, downing half the cold dark liquid in one long gulp.

"Now, explain to me how one would go swimming off Betzet beach, and end up here piloting a Lebanese Patrol Boat."

"I wish I could, Sir, but I have been sworn to secrecy."

"And this Major you mentioned swore you to secrecy?"

"That would be correct."

"What if, when that call comes in, they tell us that there is no, Major Amnon?"

"Then I would have to tell you, Captain, that they are mistaken."

Captain Asher sat back in his chair, put his hands up behind his neck and laced his fingers together.

"At about sunup this morning we picked up some radio chatter. Something about a fishing boat off the coast

16

of Tyre. It sounded to me like the Lebanese Coast Guard was chasing someone. Is there anything you can tell me about that?" David leaned back, crossed his arms, and looked squarely into Captain Asher's blue eyes.

"I can tell you that it was me they were after, Captain."

That prompted the Captain to unlace his fingers and lean in against the table.

"What happened to the crew?"

"Two of them are returning the fishing boat I borrowed and two are waiting in line to collect their seventy virgins." That seemed to bring a smile to Asher's face, even though he fought hard to suppress it.

"Now start at the beginning, Specialist Stone. Tell me why you swam into Tyre."

"Sorry, Captain. You will have to ask Major Amnon that question."

Captain Asher set his jaw and his brow lowered, forming a deep furrow between his eyes.

"Have you ever spent any time in the brig, Stone?"

"No, Captain, I have not. Why?"

"Because if you don't start cooperating and tell me what's going on, I'm going to lock you up."

"Look, Captain..."

About that time, the sailor returned from the bridge and whispered something to Captain Asher, backed away from the table, and stood by at rest with the two guards.

"Thank you Corpsman Ami, you are excused."

Captain Asher got to his feet and walked over to a phone on the bulkhead. He was on the phone for close to three minutes explaining the situation and then stood silent listening for another three. Then, smiling from ear to ear, he returned the ship's phone to its cradle, turned, and walked back to the table. He was still on his feet, standing across the table from David, when he said,

"So, Specialist Stone, this must be where you tell me that I am mistaken."

"Ah, come on Captain, that's bullshit. I trained with

the Major for three months. Hell, he drove me to the beach last night."

"I don't know who drove you to that beach last night, David. I do not even know if you are who you say you are. For all I know you might be a terrorist."

"Do I look like a Muslim, Captain?"

"One does not have to be a Muslim to be a terrorist, mister Stone."

"Captain, I swam to Tyre last night from that beach. I went there to find a man whom your government very much would like to get their hands on."

"Did you find this man?"

"No, he had already left Tyre."

"And this man that my government wants, would I know his name?"

"I would imagine that you would."

"But you're sworn to secrecy so you can't tell me his name, right?"

"Captain, what's the first thing that comes to mind when you hear "Bird Of Prey?"

"All right, hold that thought, Specialist. Gentlemen, I want this room cleared right now," he ordered.

The two guards who had been standing behind David turned, ascended back up the gangway, and closed the hatch behind themselves.

Turning his attention back to David, the Captain asked,

"This bird of prey, are you sure it has left its nest?"

"I am."

"It is not good if that is true."

"But It's not so bad if you were to know where that bird is going."

"And this you know for a fact?"

"Yes, Captain. I know where he is going and how he plans to get there."

Captain Asher leaned back in his seat and said simply, "I'm listening."

"I found a map of Cairo and a three day old

Ivan Wikert

newspaper with the headline circled in red in the Falcon's room." The Captain started to ask David if he could read Arabic, but instead he asked,

"What were you doing in that bastard's room?"
"I went there to kill him."
"No one just walks into Lebanon, Specialist Stone."
David removed the roll of papers from his waistband and held them out toward the Captain. There on the table, staring up at Captain Asher, was the headline, "Peace Talks in Cairo on the Fifteenth." He moved the newspaper aside and studied the map.

"So you stole a boat so you could come back and report this to the man who uses the name of the first born son of King David?"

"That's right, Captain. I commandeered a small fishing boat so I could get back to Israel, report what I found out, get some clothes, money and a passport, and then go after the Falcon."

"Well, Specialist Stone, what I see here is not enough to convince me that the Falcon is on his way to Cairo."

"His wife confirmed it, Captain."

"His wife? You spoke to the Falcon's wife and she told you where he was going?"

"That's right, Captain, and then the fourteen year old child bride asked me to kill her."

Captain Asher did not respond. He just stared across the table with a look that said, what did you just say?

"So, Captain, why don't you just put me ashore and let me finish what I came here to do?"

"Did you kill her?"

"No, Captain, I'm not a monster. Now how about it, will you put me ashore?"

"No, Specialist Stone. I cannot do that. What I can do is take you to Tel Aviv. You see, I don't have the authority to just put you ashore."

"Then tell me who does."

19

"Someone with more stars on his shoulder than I."

The Captain pushed his chair way from the table and stood up.

"Follow me to the bridge, Specialist Stone. We are going to Tel Aviv so you can run all this by my Commander."

David pushed away from his side of the steel table and fell in behind the Captain. Captain Asher opened the galley door then stopped, blocking the opening.

"Here, Specialist," he said, handing the twenty-two caliber weapon back to him. "I hope you understand if I hold onto the clip until we sort this all out."

"That's fine, Captain. I have four more just like it strapped to the inside of my leg." Captain Asher's brow furrowed again briefly, and then he smiled.

"Come on Specialist; let's get you to Tel Aviv."

The Captain directed the fifty-five footer to turn back to port, and the helmsman set a direct course for Tel Aviv.

The blue water curled away from the bow, spreading a blanket of white foam to both the port and starboard side. The big twin engines made their presence known, sending a steady vibration throughout the steel hull.

The Captain radioed ahead, telling his commander, without revealing too much over the open airways, about the United States Navy Seal he had intercepted, and suggested that Israeli Intelligence be called in. From high atop the ship's bridge David watched the Israeli coastline off the port side, and the line of gray Navy ships to starboard. It was not until the Coast Guard Cutter was well under way that Captain Asher suggested they go below and get something to eat.

"I thought you would never ask, Captain. I haven't had a bite since I went into the water yesterday."

Captain Asher had already summoned the cook to the galley and the grill was emitting the sweet smell of hamburgers cooking.

Another four hours had passed, and the ship had made three more stops that required Captain Asher's presence on deck. David had returned to the bridge to watch as four more vessels were boarded and searched. The sun had gone into hiding and the lights of Tel Aviv came into view off the bow. The deck hands had scrambled to make ready for docking, and it was not long before the ship's engines slowed. They had entered the naval yard east of Tel Aviv. The twin screws stopped and then reversed direction. Captain Asher barked orders to the First Mate, and signaled to David to follow him. They exited the bridge, making their way down to the deck and waited for the gangway to be lowered to the pier. David thought it strange that there was just one man standing by on the well-lit pier, but Captain Asher explained that the Commander thought it best to keep the matter as low key as possible. After the formalities and an exchange of salutes, Captain Asher turned to David and said,

"It was nice to have made your acquaintance, Specialist Stone; however, duty calls and I must return to my ship. Commander Omar will take it from here." David saluted, thanked Captain Asher, and then followed the Commander to a waiting vehicle.

A driver in a gray suit and sporting a hat straight out of a spy novel, was waiting with his hand on the door handle when David walked up to the passenger side of the black sedan. The driver opened the door, pointed inside, and said,

"Please get in."

David slid onto the back seat just as Commander Omar did the same from the opposite side. In the front seat was another much older man in a very expensive white suit, topped off with a brown leather gangster-style hat. His hair was beyond gray, leaning more toward white, causing his dark, thick-rimmed glasses to stand out in sharp contrast on his round face. The driver joined the older man in the front seat, and the black sedan sped away through the streets of Tel Aviv.

"So, Specialist Stone, what is your story,"
Commander Omar asked.

David had just begun to explain when the driver
brought the sedan to a stop at a guard shack. He handed
something out the window to an armed guard, and after a
second or two, they were inside the base.

"You were saying," Omar said.

David continued from where he had left off, but was
cut short again when the vehicle stopped a second time
inside a large empty hangar.

"Give us a few minutes, Sid," The older man in the
front seat said. The driver stepped out, closed the door
and walked away. Then the old man shifted his weight to
turn in his seat.

"Commander, if you do not mind I would like to
speak to Specialist Stone in private." Without a word,
Commander Omar opened his door, stepped out of the
vehicle and walked away.

"And now, Specialist Stone, I would like for you to
start at the very beginning. Go slowly, and leave nothing
out."

"Can I ask who you are?"

"My Name is Sol Kline. I am head of operations for
the Mossad."

David started at the beginning and explained why
he was in Israel, how he knew that the Falcon was on his
way to Cairo, and what he believed the terrorist was
planning. He handed the Major General the copy of the
As-Safir and the piece of paper with the name of the ship.

The man in the thousand dollar white suit, sat
quietly for a minute or two after David had completed his
story.

"If you're right about all this, our favorite terrorist
may have just signed his death warrant."

"I'm right, mister Kline."

"My title is Major General Kline, Specialist Stone.
we call civilians mister. Now, to finish my thoughts; how
can I be sure that you are who you say you are, Specialist

Ivan Wikert

Stone? I have never heard of this Major Amnon or any covert organization inside Israel, so I really need for you to convince me that you are who you say you are."

"Think about it, Major General. Why would I make this up?"

"I don't know, Stone. Maybe you want to get close to our Prime Minister."

"I had no idea the Prime Minister of Israel would be on the Sea Eagle."

Sol Kline laughed out loud, and said,

"Good point, Specialist, Stone. Damn good point."

"So, Stone, if you were me, what would you do next?"

"Well, Major General, the first thing I would do would be to try and locate the Sea Eagle."

"Then what?"

"Then I would sink her. I mean, if I were you, and had the entire Israeli Air Force at my disposal, that is."

"Not a bad idea, Stone. The part about locating the ship works for me; however, the sinking part is not so good. It is a certainty that people would ask questions. We should just stick with finding that ship for now, I think."

"Okay, why don't you locate the Sea Eagle, and get me on board?"

"Or, I could locate the Sea Eagle and drop in a team of our Commandos to take him out."

"Or, you could save yourself a lot of time and trouble and drop me in. I guarantee you that you will get the same result." At that point Sol Kline shifted in his seat again, looked David directly in the eyes, smiled, and said,

"Are you that good, Specialist Stone?"

"Yes, I am that good, Major General."

The old man hesitated for a minute, then smiled again and said,

"Why the hell not, Stone?"

"Good. So what are we doing hanging around here? Let's go kill us a terrorist," David said, with a look that was all business.

At that point, Sol Kline took out his cell phone and dialed a ten-digit number.

"Hello. How is my little girl," he asked. After a brief pause, he said.

"That's nice, my dear. Listen Anali, your brother David is flying to Alexandria to spend a couple of days with you."

Again, he paused and it was obvious he was listening.

"Anali, there is a strong possibility that the bird you have been waiting for is on its way to Cairo." Continuing, he said,

"Yes, my dear, that is good news. You should look for it to arrive where you are soon. I am told that it has already been shipped via a ship named the Sea Eagle. Perhaps you have heard of it." Again, he paused briefly.

"Yes, my dear, and if it arrives before your brother does, you should keep an eye on it."

He paused again and said,

"No, my dear, wait until your brother arrives. He will go with you and help you resolve the problem."

After one final pause he said,

"Yes, David will have his cell phone and you can call him when he arrives at Alexandria International. I will have Bayla call you with his flight information. Goodnight my dear."

"Who is Anali," David asked.

"She is a Major in the Mossad, and she is in Alexandria. She has been attending the American University and works part time as a secretary for Egypt's Ministry of Defense. If the Sea Eagle is there, she will find it."

"I really don't need any help. I like working alone."

"Do you have any idea what the Falcon looks like, David?"

"I've seen the composite and I know he's a butt-ugly Son-of-a-Bitch with a scar on the left side of his face."

"You can thank Anali for the composite. She is the

only person I know who can positively identify him."

"But why Alexandria? The Sea Eagle could be anywhere."

"Because if you're a terrorist on board a ship, and you want to get to Cairo, it is the closest, and most plausible route."

"Let's try to find the ship before it gets to Alexandria, Major General, and before we have to involve your female Agent."

"David, if you want my help, you will work with that female Agent because I am sticking my neck out in trusting a total stranger. Trust me, David, Anali knows her way around Alexandria and Cairo very well."

"But why risk getting her killed? Especially when I work better alone?"

"She knows the risks, David. Trust me on this, or I'll send in that commando unit I mentioned earlier."

"All right, Major General, but if she slows me down, she's on her own."

The Major General touched his hand to the horn to signal the Commander and his driver.

"Keep this between the two of us, David. The fewer people who know about this, the better."

The driver slipped back in behind the wheel and the commander returned to the back seat beside David.

"Drive us to the airport, Sid," Sol directed.

The sedan rolled out of the hangar, and this time was waved through the guard post without having to stop. The driver turned right, heading back the way they came through the streets of Tel Aviv. Sol Kline was on the phone with someone most of the way. When the car came to a stop again the driver had pulled in behind a very large, unmarked white van.

"Come with me, Specialist Stone, we have work to do. Sid, return the Commander to his office, his home, or wherever he wishes to go. Then come back here."

Inside the van were two men, a woman, and electronic equipment from wall to wall. The woman asked

25

David to take a seat and then snapped off two pictures in rapid succession. Then she handed the camera to one of her male counterparts and said,

"Please place your index finger on this screen, mister David Dupia."

He did what she asked without question, then sat back and watched as they gave birth to Anali's brother in cyberspace. Then, from her laptop, she printed the information onto a Canadian passport. From another machine they produced a Visa and a Master card.

The woman, who Sol Kline called Bayla, placed the cards, passport and some cash inside a leather bi-fold wallet and handed it to David.

"Please give me your weapon and the knife you have concealed in your right pant leg," she then requested.

David gave her a look, and said,

"No way lady, they go where I go."

"Yes, David they go where you go, but inside your carry on, a soon to be revealed leather bag. When you leave here you will go through the door marked El Al. It is right outside of this vehicle. You will walk across the tarmac to a private jet. When you land in Alexandria, you will not go through customs. There will be a man on the plane with you. He knows nothing about your mission, but he will get you safely off the runway and onto the street."

Bayla then produced a cell phone from a desk drawer and said,

"Take this cell phone, Specialist Stone. You will be contacted when you get to Cairo. Now please strip."

"I beg your pardon," he replied.

"Take off your clothes and put these on. You can't turn up on the streets of Cairo dressed like a Commando."

"But I'm not wearing any skivvies."

"I'll turn around then. Just get to it, David. Your plane is waiting."

David Stone stepped up into the van wearing the dark green sweats, carrying his weapons, and nothing else. *David Dupia* stepped out of the van wearing a flowered, short sleeved shirt, knee length tan cargo pants, a bright red Canadian Rockies ball cap, and carrying a leather bag containing a change of Canadian-labeled clothes and his weapons.

The door was marked EXIT ONLY and was unlocked. It opened inward, giving him access to the field beyond the terminal. The jet's engines were beginning to whine when he jogged across the tarmac, and just as he stepped up into the cabin, the steps rose up behind him in the form of a door. The 31A Lear Jet began to roll before he had gotten fully situated, and taxied away from the hangar. It was airborne in seconds and leveled out over the Mediterranean Sea. The small cabin accommodated six passengers and was full to capacity, seating five men in traditional Egyptian Galabyas complete with a Fez, and David in the back seat on the right side.

The aircraft had only been airborne for ten minutes before banking left. The engines quieted and then the jet began its descent. The pilot's voice came over the loud speaker and, in Arabic, he instructed them to buckle up.

The six-passenger jet banked again just before the wheels touched down. The flight lasted just under sixteen minutes from take off to landing, and another six minutes to taxi back to the terminal. After it came to a stop and the door opened, one by one the men stood up. Then, beginning with the front row, the passengers deplaned. When it was David's turn, the man who had been seated quietly across the isle held out his hand.

"Please sit down, my Canadian friend. This is not where you get off," he explained in broken English.

David reversed direction and settled back into his seat. The jet's engines powered back up and they began to move. There was radio chatter coming from up front as the pilot requested a runway, and when the small jet turned again, the door opened.

"This is where you get off, my friend. Cross the sand there," the stranger said pointing the way. "Double back to the terminal and wait. God be with you."

27

"You mean, Allah, don't you?" The man smiled, his white teeth standing out through his full black beard.

"*Shalom*, my friend."

The plane had dropped David off a good half mile from the terminal, and then gathered the speed to take off. The night sky was full of stars, and the sun had been gone for hours; yet the heat remained intense.

David could see the light poles that lined the sidewalk along the edge of the roadway. The soft desert sand shifted beneath his feet as he made his way to the two-lane and then turned east toward the terminal. He watched three airliners lift off and two land before he reached the front of the terminal building. He was relieved when he walked in through the automatic doors into the air-conditioned building.

El Nouzha was Alexandria's International Airport. There were two runways servicing flights from all over the world. Yet, as terminals go, the one David found himself standing in was not very large.

It was after 10:00 pm, and there were very few people in the lobby. There were five ticket counters on the right side, but only one that was open for business. To David's left, three security guards had gathered in an open lounge watching a soccer match on television. He walked the short distance between the entrance and the lounge, picked out a seat, and sat down where he could watch the entrance.

Fifteen minutes passed before two of the guards left the lounge and started preparing for an incoming flight. It was another ten minutes before the cell phone in his breast pocket vibrated.

"Hello," he answered.

"David, walk over to the entrance and keep your cell phone to your ear so that I will know you," a woman's soft voice said.

He looked around the terminal and said,

"All right, but I'm the only one here." Just as he reached the doors, a loud speaker announced the arrival of a flight from Cairo. David turned his back on the doors to see the first of many passengers come into view.

"David?" He heard in the same soft feminine tone.

He turned around, facing the now open doors, to see a very pretty young woman about five feet, five inches tall. She had very dark brown hair that was cut just above her shoulders, olive skin, and beautiful big brown almond-shaped eyes. She was dressed in a traditional Egyptian full-length, white linen Galabya that left nothing uncovered above the ankles.

Before he had fully taken in her picture she threw her arms around his neck and kissed him.

"I am so glad to see you, brother," she said, releasing her strong grip from his neck.

"How are you, Anali? It's been a while."

She laughed and said,

"Yes brother, David, I would say that it has. Come, my car is just outside. We must get you settled; there is a lot for us to catch up on."

He followed her out into the hot night air to the curb, and then across the busy street to a white, older model Saab.

"Get in," she instructed.

The engine perked up, and the air-conditioning began to struggle against the African heat.

"Tell me, David, how can you be sure that the Falcon is on his way to Alexandria?"

"I found a newspaper with the headline, "Peace Talks To Begin In Cairo On The Fourteenth," and the name of the ship in his room."

"You were in the Falcon's room? Why?"

"To kill him." She turned her eyes away from the road and looked into the eyes of her make-believe brother.

"I was told that the Falcon lives among the Hezbollah leaders in Tyre."

"That's true."

"And you were there?"

"Yes, I was there."

29

"Alone?"

"Yes."

"Why would you do that?"

"Like I said, Anali, I went there to kill The Falcon."

"Will you know that son of a dog when you see him?"

"No, Anali, but he will be on the Sea Eagle, and he's heading for Cairo. I'll get him."

"I have seen his face, David. So if he is coming as you say, I will help you get him."

The front end of the car bounced through a swale at the side of the road when Anali turned into a narrow alley. The sound of the pipes echoed off the walls of the tall sandstone buildings when she caught a lower gear, sped up again, and then turned left at the next cross street. She applied more pressure to the throttle and grabbed a taller gear. The Saab's four-cylinder engine was roaring like a big cat as they sped along the deserted street, and then quickly calmed down to a purr as she turned into a parking lot.

"Welcome to my home, David."

She opened the driver's side door and slid out. The building was a six-story complex overlooking the Port of Alexandria.

"Up there, David," she said, pointing to a darkened window on the fifth floor. "You will be able to see every ship that enters the port."

She opened the trunk lid allowing David to grab his leather bag, then closed it and led the way up the walkway to the front door. She gained access by punching in a five-letter code in a box beside the door and led the way up the five flights of narrow stairs.

Her apartment consisted of three rooms; a small bedroom, an even smaller bathroom, and a combination kitchen/living room that opened up onto a balcony.

David walked to the glass French doors overlooking the parking lot below and the vast seaport of Alexandria.

"You can open the doors, David. The sea breeze

will feel good," she said before disappearing into the bedroom.

The glass doors opened inward, and the fresh night air rushed in to fill the room. David stepped out onto the balcony and took an unobstructed look at the Egyptian night. Streetlights marked the contour of the roadway that curved gently around, following the harbor's long shoreline. A gentle breeze cooled off the humid night. Date palms swayed in the light sea breeze, and out beyond the line of trees, scattered out on the surface of the dark water, were the lights of many anchored vessels shining back toward the city.

David was still leaning on the handrail, looking out over the Mediterranean when Anali returned to the living area. She made a stop at the refrigerator and turned off the lights behind her before walking out to join him on the balcony.

"It is hard to imagine that it was a hundred degrees at two O'clock this afternoon," she said, after handing the ice-cold container to her guest. His hand reached for the bottle, but his eyes found Anali. She was no longer wearing the long white Galabya that covered her from neck to toe. She had shed the typical Egyptian attire for a pair of loose-fitting white shorts and a green sleeveless cotton shirt. The shorts were cut like boxers and hung half way to her knees. The light cotton shirt stopped five or six inches above her waistline.

She sat down in one of the two deck chairs and said,

"So, David Dupia, who are you really? I lived in Canada, and you don't sound like any Canadian I have ever met."

"I'm from sunny California, Anali."

"I thought as much. How did you get involved in this?" He smiled and said,

"Would you believe I drew the short straw?"

"Is that what you would like me to believe, David?"

"Tell me, Anali, why are you part of this?"

31

She was quiet briefly, and then answered,

"When I was nine years old my father was killed by a suicide bomber in Cashmere, India. My mother is French Canadian and, after my father was killed, we returned to Montréal. At that point, David had to stop her.

"I always figured that all Mossad Agents were Israeli. You know, Jewish."

"Well, you figured wrong, David. Most are, but not all."

"All right, so how did a girl from Montréal end up spying for the Mossad?"

"Have you ever been to Canada, David?"

"No, never have."

"Well, there are a lot of Muslims in Montréal, and when you grow up and go to school with them, you learn quickly who and what they are really all about."

"And what are they all about, Anali?"

"Let me just say that I never met a Muslim who didn't secretly pray for the destruction of Israel and the United States."

"So, because you grew up around Muslims you just decided to come to the aid of their enemy?"

"No, David, I was a gymnast in high school and I tried out for the Canadian Olympic team my senior year. In the spring of 2004 when I visited Israel with my team to compete against the Jewish State's team, I witnessed a terrorist attack. That was the day that changed my life forever. Three of we girls where sitting in a sidewalk café in Jerusalem having lunch. I was sitting in the chair facing the street, so I witnessed this car pull up and stop directly across the street. A man dressed in a white suit exited from the driver's side and walked straight across the street and into the café. I will never forget that man's face for as long as I live."

"The Falcon," David asked.

"Yes. His eyes were black, and when he saw me watching him he glared at me as if he were trying to melt my soul. His face was pock-marked and he had an ugly scar from the bridge of his nose to his right ear," she said, running her right index finger across her own face.

The lighting was dim on the balcony but David was able to make out her gesture, and he heard the intensity in her voice as she continued,

"He walked past our table and sat down at an empty one near the door leading inside the café; and then perhaps two minutes later the car exploded. The blast knocked me over backwards and the table came crashing down on top of me. The smoke and heat from the blast swept through the café and I could hear people all around me screaming. Then, for some reason I looked back to where the strange man had been sitting. I will never forget the look of satisfaction on the son of a dog's ugly face. He had walked inside the building before detonating his bomb, and had just returned to the opening to survey his dirty work when I looked up at him. The bastard smiled, pointed his finger at me and dropped his thumb. You know, as if his hand were a pistol, and he had pulled the trigger. Two of my teammates were dead and another badly wounded. All in all, the Falcon left seven people dead that afternoon, and thirty or more wounded."

"So what did you decide to do?"

"I decided to help the police by giving them a description of the bomber. One thing led to another and before I knew it, I was at a military base training to be a spy."

"If no one knew what the Falcon looked like, how sure are you that the man you saw that day was him?"

"Because the son of a dog left his calling card. He removed a fired clay statue of a Falcon from the pocket of his suit coat and put it down next to me on the floor."

It was quiet for a spell and then Anali asked,

"So, now it's your turn, David. Why are you here working for the Mossad?

"I told you, Anali, I drew the short straw."

Without a word, she stood up and stormed back inside her dark apartment. He knew without asking that she was upset with him, so he got to his feet and followed her. There was fire in her big brown eyes when the lights came on in the kitchen.

"You Americans make me sick. You come here and make a joke of the war on terror."

"Anali, I'm sorry. I didn't mean to upset you. I assure you that I take my assignment very seriously."

"Then answer my question, damn you. Why are you here?"

"Well, Anali my name is David Stone. I'm here for the same reason you are. I volunteered to eliminate Ahmed Ali Mohammed."

"Good. Why didn't you just say that in the first place, David?"

"Because I'm still not used to the idea of a partner, Anali."

"Then go home. I'll find the Sea Eagle myself, and I'll kill that murdering dog."

"When was the last time you killed anyone, Anali?" If looks could kill, the one she gave him would have rendered him dead at that point.

"There is always a first time, David. How many people have you actually killed?"

"Four in the last twenty-four hours. Before that, I'm not sure."

"Four in the last twenty-four hours? Are you serious," she asked, questioning his statement.

David looked at his watch and counted back in his head.

"No, I was wrong, Anali; the count is four in the last *twenty* hours."

He explained to her about his six-hour swim into Tyre, and all that had transpired between 1:30 am that morning and the present time. After he had explained everything, all she had to say was,

"That son of a dog bought a fourteen year old girl to be his third wife. I would like to ask a favor of you, David," she continued.

"Ask away, Anali."

"When we find the evil one, I would like to be the one who sends him to hell. I would like very much to smile down at him, point my weapon at his ugly face and pull the trigger."

He did not have to think about what she had asked for very long before an answer came to mind, and that answer was no; however, what he said instead was,

"Anali, I have no problem with you wanting to get vengeance for your friends. My problem is, are you up to the task?"

"Don't forget about my father and every other man, woman and child killed by that evil son of a dog. I am not only up to the task; I have four years of my life invested in getting this evil one. So, like it or not, David Stone, you have a partner."

He smiled and looked the pretty little spy in the eyes.

"You sure have built up a lot of hate for that one Muslim extremist."

"I think terrorists are the lowest life form on earth, David, but there is a special place in hell for the Falcon."

"Why don't we find him first, Anali? Then, if it doesn't compromise my mission, you can have the first shot."

"Fair enough, David. Are you hungry? I have some bread and cheese in the fridge, and there might even be a bottle of wine to wash it down with."

"Sounds good."

When she walked over to the refrigerator, he could not help but notice her legs; they were the legs of a long-distance runner.

"Do you work out, Anali?"

"What do you mean," she asked as she returned with the bread, cheese, and the wine.

"How do you stay in shape?"

"Oh, you know, sit ups, chin ups - that sort of stuff. I have a treadmill in the bedroom, and I have been known to slip out early in the morning and jog through the back streets. Why do you ask?"

"It's just that you seem to be in very good shape."

"Thank you, I try."

She took a knife and bread board off the counter as he sat down at the small breakfast counter and she stood on the kitchen side while they shared the French bread and goat cheese. When they had finished off most of both, she returned what little was left to the refrigerator.

David walked back to the balcony where the night air was the coolest and leaned against the railing. When Anali finished up in the kitchen, she turned out the light and joined him.

"How long have you been here in Alexandria, Anali?"

"Three years, two months and, at midnight tonight, four days."

"Sol Kline said that you're a student?"

"That's my cover. I take classes at the American University."

"What's your major? Pardon the pun."

"History. I thought that if I ever get tired of spying, I would teach."

"So teacher, tell me something about this city."

"All right, David. Alexander the Great founded Alexandria in 334 B.C. At the time, this city was the Capital of Egypt. The Muslim's conquered the city in 641 A.D. and a new Capital was founded at Fustat. Fustat is now part of Cairo. Would you like to hear more?"

"Sure, why not."

"Alexandria is the second largest city in Egypt with over four million residents. The city extends thirty-two kilometers along the coast, and is called the Pearl Of The Mediterranean. Over eighty percent of all Egypt's imports and exports come in and go out from here. Look over there," she said, pointing to a lighthouse. "That is one of the seven wonders of the ancient world. It was built as a landmark between 285 and 247 B.C. on Pharo's Island.

Ptolemy I Soter, Egypt's first Macedonian Ruler reconstructed it as a lighthouse in the third century B.C.. It has been rebuilt three times after being damaged by earthquakes. Under the city are the Catacombs of Kom El Shoqafa; some call them Mounds of Shards. The Mounds were uncovered in 1900 when a donkey fell into an access shaft. There are Alexandrian tombs, statues, and archaeological objects dating back to the Pharaonic Funeral Cult, or the Middle Ages. To date, three Sarcophagi have been found. Have you had enough, David?"

"No, I'd like to hear more, but it is late. Maybe we could continue this tomorrow."

"You're right, it is getting late and we should get up early, David. We have a ship to find.

He followed her back inside the apartment.

"You can have the couch. It is much cooler out here."

"The couch will do just fine, Anali. Thank you."

When she disappeared into her bedroom, David turned and walked back out onto the balcony, sat down in the chair he had occupied earlier, and put his feet up in the other one. It had cooled down in the living room, but it was even cooler out in the open air. He fell asleep and spent the rest of the night with his head resting against the wall, stretched out between the two chairs.

Chapter 3

The hot African sun slipped quietly up into the sky over the Sudan, and began its journey across the vast, Sahara desert. All along the waterfront, the shadows of the buildings quickly stretched out across the harbor, and then slowly began to withdraw from the Mediterranean Sea. The darkness was swept away to reveal the emerald green surface of Alexandria's Seaport.

David was awake, but still holding fast to his position overlooking the gulf when Anali emerged from her bedroom. She had showered, dressed in a light cotton robe, and was drying her hair with a towel.

"You are welcome to the bathroom now, David," she said without coming all the way out onto the balcony.

"Good Morning, Anali. Thank you, I think I will."

He stood up, stretched, and walked in off the balcony. The warm water was refreshing and he lingered to remove the two-day-old dry salt residue from his pores.

Anali had set up a telescope on the balcony overlooking the harbor, and while David was in the shower, she began scanning the ships across the way.

The Sea Eagle had come in on the midnight tide, and was being held just beyond the jetty by tugboats. She had turned her attention from the name on the ship's bow to the human forms on her deck, hoping to catch a glimpse of the Falcon when she heard David coming from the bathroom. He had dried himself off and wrapped one of her towels around his waist. He was on his way to where he had dropped his bag when he heard her say,

"Come quick David! You must see this." He walked out onto the balcony, leaned in and covered the eyepiece with his right eye.

"Good job, Anali. Maybe we should get down to the

dock before our bird comes ashore."

"Give me two minutes to change and we can go; oh, and David, it looks like you're in pretty good shape yourself," she said before turning to go back inside.

David opened his bag and let the towel around his waist fall to the floor, and stepped into the only long pair of pants his Israeli friends had packed for him. Then he slipped a loose fitting short sleeved shirt over his head.

Anali emerged from her bedroom still in the process of buttoning her white cotton blouse to go with the light blue skirt she was wearing.

"I am ready when you are, David," she said, lifting her bag to her shoulder.

He clipped his holster to his waistband in the middle of his back and pulled his shirttail down to conceal it.

"After you, sis." he said in jest.

She smiled and walked past him out into the hallway, then he followed her down the stairs and out though the door to the parking lot.

The white Saab rolled slowly to a stop at a stop sign then turned left, proceeding south along the waterfront. There was a steady line of flatbed trucks in the right hand lane, and men crowded the sidewalk along the seawall, making their way to work on the docks.

The Sea Eagle was still in the control of the tugs, and lay about fifty yards offshore when Anali pulled into a parking space directly across from the gates.

"Now we wait," she said after cutting the engine.

The sun had come up over the high rises, and it was beginning to get hot when the powerful tugs pushed the ship into position alongside the dock under the cargo cranes.

The deck immediately came alive with passengers and crew. The gangways were moved into place, allowing the workers a way up and passengers a way down. Anali leaned forward in anticipation when the first wave of passengers came out through the wide-open gates, but then relaxed when she was sure the Falcon was not among them.

She opened her bag, removed her Israeli Arms nine millimeter from inside, and pulled back on the slide.

"If the Falcon shows himself, David I will get out of the car and walk toward him. He will not be suspicious of a woman. When I shoot him you should get out and walk away."

"Whoa, Anali. If the Falcon comes out through that gate we will follow him and his men out where there are fewer people around."

"He can not be allowed to escape, David."

"Anali, we have the advantage. Trust me; the bastard does not know we're onto him. He won't get away this time."

They were still discussing the hypothetical when Anali stopped talking and pointed to a group of men coming across the street. Ahmed Ali Muhammad and three comrades were in the crosswalk headed straight for their location.

"There's that ugly son of a dog!" she exclaimed as she reached for the weapon she had just minutes earlier placed back in her bag. David placed his hand on her wrist and said,

"Wait, Anali. Let's see where they're going."

The Falcon and his men all looked right at the young couple sitting in the Saab, and Ahmed had an evil grin on his face. He turned his head as he walked by and kept his black eyes trained on Anali's face.

The Falcon sported a full, but well kept beard. His high cheeks bore deep pockmarks, and just as Anali had said, he had a scar that ran from the bridge of his unusually large roman nose, across his high cheekbone and ended behind his left ear.

She snarled and spit,

"I will cut your heart out, you dog." Her eyes followed the evil one as he continued past the Saab.

Ahmed and the three men with him were all

dressed in dark blue suits, no ties, white shoes, and had Arafat style turbans on their heads. They stopped briefly at the island in the middle of the busy street, waiting for the traffic to clear, and then continued on to the other side.

A man in a traditional white Galabya topped off with a red Fez was leaning against the front fender of a white Toyota wagon just across the roadway that paralleled the Stanley Bridge. Anali turned the ignition key and started the engine.

The man who awaited their arrival had never seen the Falcon before, but was told to look for a slender man in his forties wearing the barbed wire patterned turban that symbolized the Palestinian Struggle.

"Welcome, Ahmed," said the driver, opening both the front and back doors.

"Is everything in place?"

The driver looked into the black eyes of the notorious killer.

"Yes, Sir. Would you do me the honor," he asked, gesturing for Ahmed to take the front passenger seat. Ahmed did not respond and chose the backseat instead, sliding in and across to the window on the driver's side.

A much younger man ducked under the driver's arm, sat down in the front seat, and closed the door without a word. The other two joined Ahmed in the back seat. The younger man's eyes followed the driver as he made his way around the car, and when he was inside and the door was pulled shut, he asked,

"Is the money in here?" referring to a briefcase between the front bucket seats.

"Yes it is."

"And the weapons, where are they?"

"In the back, under a blanket."

"Then drive," the young man ordered. The white Toyota wagon pulled out from the curb, making a U-turn across traffic, and sped off along 26th Of July Avenue, away from Eastern Harbor.

Anali pushed the gas peddle to the floor, scattering

the crowd as she zeroed in on the tail end of the white
Toyota.

"Back off just a little, Anali. We don't want them to
know we're following them," David suggested. She backed
off enough to avoid suspicion, but stayed close enough
behind so that she would not lose them at a light.

The four terrorist's and the Egyptian driver turned
right at the next light, and away from the sea, through the
busy streets of Alexandria.

It was not long before the wide, well kept streets of
the city gave way, and the Toyota was on the two-lane
highway headed toward Cairo. The city was behind them
now, and all that remained were a few scattered fort-like
estates and desert sand.

The wagon's brake lights flashed and the vehicle
slowed down and came to a stop in front of a gated
compound. Two men appeared from inside and opened
the gates, clearing the way for the Toyota to enter. The
vehicle slowly turned in through two open gates into a well-
kept and equally guarded compound at the edge of the
great sea of sand.

Anali slowed her Saab to a crawl and rolled slowly
past the open gates. David counted seven men; Ahmed,
his three followers, and the Egyptian driver, who had
already exited the Toyota and were moving quickly away
from the vehicle toward the building. The two guards who
had opened the gates, were armed with automatic
weapons, and were dressed like Palestinians. They wore
long shirts or Thobe's, baggy cotton pants called Sirwal's,
and white turbans, with patterned black lines depicting
barbed wire.

The Saab rolled to a stop on the side of the road,
less than forty yards from the compound's south corner.

"I counted seven men, Anali."

"The two Arabs are still watching us, David," she
said with her eyes trained on her rear view mirror.

"We should wait a few minutes and see if they
lose interest in us; and if they do, we should take a walk

around the compound and see if there is another way in."

"Maybe if I were to walk to the gate and draw their attention you could get behind them."

David rolled down his window and adjusted the rear view mirror on his side so that he could see what she was looking at. The guards stood there for another five minutes before walking back inside and closing the gates.

"Anali, let's give it another five minutes or so, and then when we get out of the car I'll open the hood. Maybe if they think we're broke down they'll forget about us."

While David and Anali waited out the five minutes, one of the guards appeared on the rooftop above the house where Ahmed and his men were. Anali was the first to notice him when she stepped out of the Saab.

"Look up there on the roof, David. So much for them forgetting about us." He opened the hood and Anali walked around to the back of the car to join him.

"We might as well just walk right up to the gates and take them straight away, David." He turned and looked the situation over one more time and said,

"Why not?"

Chapter 4

Inside the desert compound, behind closed doors, the four terrorists were relaxing under the refrigerated air conditioning in the living room. Ahmed had sent the driver back out to the car with orders to bring the weapons inside. Askari was Ahmed's most trusted and loyal friend. His first name meant soldier in Arabic. He was a half head shorter, twenty pounds heavier, and ten years younger than the man he followed. He was clean-shaven and light skinned, and could pass for a westerner. The youngest was Seleh, Ahmed's oldest of seven children. He would turn fifteen in three months time. He was three inches shorter and twenty pounds lighter than Ahmed, but favored his father quite a bit. The fourth man was Al Zaabi Hussan. He was an Egyptian, and knew Cairo like the back of his hand. He had family living in the old city west of where the talks were scheduled to take place. His younger brother, Ali, was sitting on the weapon they planned to use to bring down the Israeli Prime Minister's plane. The men all made themselves comfortable on throws in the living area and waited for the driver to return from the car with the weapons.

"Father, when will we leave for Cairo," Seleh asked.

"We will wait for darkness, my son."

"We should get something to eat and then rest until sundown. Not even camels move when the sun is in the sky," added Al Zaabi.

The driver opened the front door and came in carrying a weighted suitcase. He put it down on a small table in the center of the room and opened it up to reveal an assortment of handguns.

"I pray that these are to your liking," he said.

Seleh quickly picked up the gun case and moved from man to man, waiting for each to choose, then picked a forty-five caliber British made revolver for himself.

"I will kill the Infidels," he exclaimed, waving the revolver over his head.

"Put the weapon down, my son, or you will not be going with us," snapped Ahmed.

"Yes father, I am sorry."

"You must act like a man, Seleh, or I will send you back to your mother."

"I will make you proud, father."

"Put the forty-five back in the case, Seleh, we will all carry one of these," Ahmed said, holding up a three-eighty automatic.

"Driver, come here." he barked.

"Rashad is my name," said the driver.

"Rashad, how much for the wagon?"

"I do not know what you mean, Sir."

"How much money do you need to replace your car?"

"I ..."

"Here, five thousand should be enough," he said, cutting Rashad off.

"That is very kind of Ahmed," he said, bowing slightly at the waist.

"You can thank the Syrians. They have been very generous."

"I will have my woman fix you something. You should eat before you go."

"Yes, that would be fine. And some wine, if you please."

Rashad disappeared through a draped doorway, and he said,

"Asilah, we have guests. Prepare them something to eat."

Ahmed summoned them all around the small table and began to rehash their plan. He began with a diatribe on how what they were planning to do was Allah's will, and the rewards that would come to all of them when they were successful.

Al Zaabi spoke of more earthly and pertinent matters, such as the weapon that his brother held for them and the place from where their plan would be carried out. Askari listened while he loaded clips with ammunition, and Seleh sat silently.

The compound was surrounded on all four sides by a sea of wind-rippled sand. The prevailing winds had pushed drifts against the south wall almost eight feet high, but all along the highway in front of the compound had been cleared.

One of the guards remained near the front gates and, although David and Anali couldn't see him, they knew he was there. They could see the one on the roof and they knew he was still keeping an eye on them.

"Are you ready, Anali?"

"I am ready, David."

"Then let's go kill us a terrorist."

She slipped her nine millimeter back into her bag but kept her hand on the weapon, as they continued walking slowly back in the direction of the compound. They were walking side by side, keeping to the edge of the gravel road.

The guard on the roof never took his eyes off them, and it was not until the eight-foot high wall blocked his view that he finally lost sight of them.

He trained his eyes on the gates waiting for the couple to walk by, and when he thought enough time had passed, and they had not appeared, he yelled down to the other guard near the gate.

David and Anali had moved off the side of the road when they knew he could not see them and stopped in the shade. He removed his twenty-two caliber automatic from his waistband when they were just ten feet from the gates, knowing that any minute the guard nearest the gate would come out to check on the intruders.

The hinges squeaked, then one of the gates

opened outward and a single guard appeared.

"You must leave this place, now," the Arab man yelled in his native tongue.

David raised his hands up shoulder high and moved toward the guard. The guard moved closer, motioning with the business end of his AK-47 assault rifle.

"You must go now!" He barked again.

Anali followed David's lead. She noticed that he had returned his weapon to his waistband so she stepped out to his left, but kept her right hand inside her bag, finger on the trigger, and the barrel pointed toward the advancing guard.

"We were just resting in the shade of your wall," David explained, in Arabic.

"You can not rest here. Go away with you," the guard again commanded.

The man took a couple of steps forward and could no longer be seen by his partner on the rooftop. David's hands were still in the air. The guard took two more steps forward, closing the distance between himself and David to three feet.

David's hands were still above his shoulders when the guard attempted to poke him in the chest with the barrel of his weapon. What happened next happened so fast that Anali, and most definitely the guard, never saw it coming.

David's right hand closed quickly around the round steel barrel, pushing it to one side. At the same time, with his open left hand he struck the man's windpipe, and then his hand closed around the guard's throat. He gasped for air as his head was slammed against the sandstone wall. David's powerful grip had cut the blood supply to his brain, rendering him totally helpless. His sandals all but came off the ground when David pushed him up against the wall. His arms dropped to his sides, and he released his grip on the AK47. David released his grip on the rifle, letting it fall to the sand at his feet. The guard closed his eyes, and stopped struggling.

His legs failed him, but David held him up until he was sure that death was certain.

Anali was quite impressed with the swift, quiet and clean manner in which her partner had eliminated the guard. She looked closely into the dead man's eyes when she bent down to retrieve the assault rifle lying next to his body.

"That's the first good Arab I've seen today."

"Let's see if we can find him some company," David said, removing his weapon from his waistband. He began moving along the wall toward the open gate. Anali followed him with the AK47 in hand, nearly stepping on his heels. David put his back flat against the wall and cautiously peered around the corner of the gate. There was no one in the courtyard between them and the house, but the guard on the roof was locked, loaded and had his eyes trained on the gates.

"Hakbar!" He yelled out to his missing comrade.

"Hakbar!" He yelled a second time.

The second time the guard shouted "Hakbar," Rashad stepped out into the open and looked up at the man on the roof.

"What is wrong," he said.

Just as he spoke and the guard on the rooftop looked down, David stepped out from behind the wall. The next sound was the bark of the twenty-two automatic, and the man on the roof stumbled, stepped back and then fell, disappearing behind the parapet.

Rashad had his back to the gate when the first shot was fired and quickly ducked down just as David fired off a second round. The bullet that was directed at the middle of his back grazed his right arm just below the shoulder. He stumbled and cried out in anguish when the small caliber bullet hit him, but somehow managed to make it back inside and close the door before David's third shot embedded itself in the wood.

Gunfire suddenly erupted from the front of the building, prompting David to quickly take cover back behind the wall. The bullets continued to fly, peppering the entrance and ricocheting off the edge of the wall and the pavement out front.

David and Anali hunkered down, and over the sound of small arms firing they could hear men yelling, car doors slamming, and then an engine start up.

"Move back!" David said prompting her to her feet.

They made a run for the corner of the compound. They had not gotten far before the front end of the white Toyota wagon struck the iron gates with enough force to snap the hinges.

There were five men inside, and the two on the passenger side were firing wildly out through the open windows.

David and Anali crouched and returned fire. The Toyota wagon served from side to side as it sped by them. As the vehicle sped away, they both stood up and emptied their clips. When the car disappeared in a cloud of dust, he looked at her and she looked at him, and then without a word they both made a mad dash for the Saab. It came to life quickly, kicking up two rooster tails of yellowish brown sand behind the spinning tires. Anali went through the gears like a professional, and the needle on the speedometer jumped quickly to eighty miles per hour.

Dust still lingered over the roadway and, as the distance between the two speeding vehicles shortened, the cloud became increasingly heavier. Anali was having trouble seeing the road, and they both knew from the boiling dust cloud that they were right on the Falcon's tail.

Without warning, the rear end of the Toyota wagon appeared. Anali let up on the throttle and touched the brakes to avoid running right up their tail pipe. David cranked his window down, stuck his weapon out into the blast of sand, and fired.

The rear window in the Toyota shattered and the tail end of the fleeing vehicle swerved to the left side of the road then back to the right. Something hit the front of the Saab hard, and again Anali backed off on the throttle.

The Falcon's Final Flight

The steering wheel started to vibrate, and then as the car slowed down more the wheel began to shake violently. The boiling dust cloud had moved on by the time the Saab rolled to a complete stop. Anali released her grip on the steering wheel and then pounded on it three times with her hands.

"Damn it! Damn it! Damn it! She exclaimed.

David opened his door and got out. He found the problem on his side of the car.

"We have a flat tire," he announced.

Anali pulled the lever that released the latch on the bonnet and then pushed her door open. The dust was still settling when she stepped out onto the road.

"I didn't hear any gunshots, David. Did you?"

"No, but these weren't here last time I looked."

He pointed to four deep dents in the front end of the Saab; one in the fender under the headlight on the driver's side, two in the front of the bonnet just above the bumper, and the fourth, the only one that penetrated, went through the blinker light into the tire on the passenger side.

"Grab the spare, David. They're getting away," she said, having already grabbed the jack.

Changing the tire took under three minutes, but they knew that at eighty miles an hour three minutes translated to five, maybe six miles.

Anali threw the jack back into the trunk, and although it was no longer of any use, David tossed the shredded tire in and slammed the lid. He was closing his door as the Saab lurched, and they were back in hot pursuit.

David released the empty clip from his weapon, letting it fall to the floorboard and quickly replaced it with a full one from his bag. Then he reached up and removed Anali's nine millimeter from the dash where she had deposited it, and began fumbling through her bag for a second clip.

The road to Cairo was a two-lane, but narrowed in spots where the drifting sand tried to reclaim its surface.

50

"Are there any crossroads where they might turn off," David asked just after he returned her fully loaded handgun to the dashboard.

"Not that I know of, and it's a hundred kilometers to the next village. The highway runs as straight as an arrow south, and eventually parallels the Nile. The road continues to parallel the river all the way to Cairo, but we can't let them make it to Cairo," she added as she gave the Saab more fuel.

One hundred kilometers is sixty-two miles and, at the speed they were traveling, it would take less than a half hour to get to the first village.

"Back there at the gate, when that guard pointed his rifle at you, how did you know?"

"How did I know what?"

"That you could do what you did, David. I never saw anything like that before."

"It's what I'm trained to do, Anali."

"Well, you do what you do very well, David Stone."

Before he could say anything in response, she let up on the gas pedal.

"I think we may have hit one of them back there, David,"

"What makes you say that?"

"Because there's something lying in the road up ahead, and there aren't any large animals out here," she said as she applied the brakes.

She brought the Saab to a stop about twenty feet away and David stepped out of the passenger side. He walked slowly, holding his weapon down but ready, to where a man dressed in a dark blue suit and white shoes lay face down in the middle of the road.

"You're right, Anali. We did hit one of them."

"Good," she answered from just a few feet away. She had also exited the vehicle and was standing right beside him.

David knelt down and placed his forefinger against the man's throat, checking for a pulse.

The Falcon's Final Flight

"This one's still alive," he said.   And then, just as he stood up, one single gunshot rang out, and Anali said simply,

"No, David, you are mistaken." David shook his head and smiled,

"I stand corrected, Anali. You get the car and I'll pull this low-life off the road."

"That's the second good Arab I've seen today, David."

The afternoon sun was punishing the Sahara's parched landscape, and the horizon became lost in a heat-wave-induced mirage.

David deposited the dead terrorist off the road in the bar ditch just as the front wheel on the passenger side of the Saab came to a stop in a puddle of fresh blood. He opened the door quickly and slipped back into the seat.

Chapter 5

Fifty kilometers from the gates of the compound on the outskirts of Alexandria, the Toyota wagon rolled slowly to a stop. All four doors flew open and everyone climbed out, and three out of the four kicked the side of the crippled vehicle.

Rashad walked around the Toyota, and after a quick study, found the problem. The vehicle had spent most of its fuel through a small twenty-two caliber hole in the side of the ten-gallon tank.

"We are out of petrol," he said, sharing the bad news with the others.

Ahmed looked back down the road, and again cursed the Infidels. He looked up into the cloudless sky, and asked Allah to strike them dead.

"There must be a village somewhere," Askari said, directing his belief to Rashad.

"Six, maybe seven kilometers further," the injured Rashad explained.

Askari returned to the Toyota passenger seat, retrieved the briefcase full of money, grabbed the extra clips for his three-eighty Remington that he had thrown into the back seat, and returned to Ahmed's side.

"It is not safe to stay on the road. We should go to the river, Ahmed," he stated.

"You are right, Askari. We will find a boat."

Rashad kept his mouth shut. He had witnessed how these men treated their friends. When the Egyptian slumped over and they realized that he had been hit, Askari simply opened the door and kicked him out of the speeding car.

Seleh argued that they should wait and ambush the Infidels. Askari argued that they should find a boat or another car and finish the mission. Ahmed agreed with his soldier. Ahmed and the three remaining terrorists left the road on the downhill side. They headed directly for the river, hoping that somewhere along the Nile they would find a vehicle or a boat to take them south to Cairo. They had traveled less than a half mile when David and Anali pulled in behind the abandoned Toyota.

Across the sea of yellowed Sudan grass, the terrain gently declined, and beyond the line of desert palms and willows, they could see the blue-green waters of the Nile rolling silently north in search of the Mediterranean.

David opened his door and stepped out. Anali removed her pistol from the dash and joined him. They both advanced slowly, considering the possibility of an ambush, until he noticed the fresh tracks in the sand leading toward the river.

"It looks like they had car trouble, Anali, and now they're on foot," he said, pointing out the footprints.

"We must go after them, David. That dog must not leave this God forsaken place alive."

"Grab whatever you want to take with you then, and let's go."

Anali grabbed her bag and slammed the driver's side door. David did the same and followed her off the road. She broke into a fast jog shortly after leaving the hard surface and, with the hot desert sun at their backs, they raced against time and the elements.

They knew that they had to be making up the distance between themselves and the terrorists and were closing fast on the river when a shot rang out. Anali went down and rolled to her left, taking cover behind a small palm tree. David turned right, picking up speed and drawing a volley of small arms fire from somewhere down by the water. Anali stood up behind the tree and returned a five round burst in the direction of the terrorists.

David disappeared into the thick stand of papyrus the terrorists were using as cover. The thin-stemmed trees were twelve feet tall, and thick enough to make moving through them difficult. When David disappeared from sight, an almost deafening silence fell over the area.

Ahmed and his men were on the move again, running south along the riverbank. Anali moved out in the open and fired three more shots into the thicket. And then when it was clear, she took off in hot pursuit.

The closer they came to the river, the taller and thicker the papyrus and desert palms became. David stopped when he heard a gunshot that came from Anali's nine millimeter. She was just a few feet from him but he could not see her.

By the time he did get to where she was standing, she had fired another six shots, and was loading another clip into her weapon. She was standing at the water's edge firing at a small boat that was no more than sixty yards away. The small outboard motor was wound tight, fighting against the Nile's strong current.

"That son of a dog is getting away," Anali exclaimed when she noticed him standing beside her.

David raised the twenty-two automatic, and took careful aim. His first shot fell short, his second splashed down just inches from the stern, and the third hit the small outboard.

The men in the small flat bottom skiff returned fire, spraying lead aimlessly. David fired four more times and then grabbed Anali, pulling her off her feet and down to the ground.

The outboard began sputtering and then quickly died. Then the wooden boat slowed and started to drift back downstream with the current.

David covered Anali with his body when Ahmed and his remaining cohorts opened fire again, but once again their volley failed to reach the river's muddy bank.

Ahmed and his band of terrorists were seventy yards offshore, drifting slowly back down river toward Alexandria in an old wooden boat that was overloaded.

In the midst of the gun battle, a large crocodile slid off the muddy shoreline, sinking beneath the blue water.

Others stirred nervously but stayed on land through it all. The Nile was home to crocodiles, hippos, anacondas, and eels that could light you up like a Christmas tree, and it was, in most places, one hundred yards wide.

"I think we just might have the Falcon cooped up, Anali." David suggested. Then he rolled away from her and sat up. "Come on, we should get moving."

They moved through the tall grass and palm trees, keeping pace with the powerless skiff. Anali stopped long enough to fire two rounds, but both fell well short of her intended target.

"I sure wish I had kept that rifle."

"That's the bad thing about nine millimeters, Anali; they just don't have enough range."

David stopped and took careful aim. He knew that his twenty-two had the range, but delivered a much smaller pill. He could not tell where his first shot went, but it caused a stir inside the boat. He fired again, and that one found a home. The boat rocked violently and all aboard attempted to duck down and hide inside the hull.

David fired again and then again, and the small wooden skiff rocked violently and all hands went over the far side. And then, as the boat drifted out of the way, they could see three of the four terrorists swimming away toward the far shoreline. The forth man was still clinging to the side of the boat.

"Looks like we're going for a swim, David,"

"Let's wait and see if they make it first. The current might just do our job for us."

"No, David we can't let him get away again."

David moved downstream watching the three terrorists fight the mighty Nile's three-point-one-million-liter-per-second flow while Anali made herself ready to swim the river. He very carefully searched the riverbank with his eyes until he saw the three men crawl out of the water on their hands and knees. The river's current had carried them close to a quarter of a mile down stream and, even from a hundred yards away, they looked like drowned rats.

Ahmed stood up and yelled something, but his voice was lost on the surface of the Nile.

David could see that he was shaking his fist in the air. He was just about to answer the Falcon's gesture by lobbing a round across the river when he noticed Anali struggling to keep her bag above the surface. She was fighting to swim the Nile with one arm, and she was losing the fight. The current had swept her off her feet, and for every foot she gained toward the far side she drifted ten feet downriver.

"Let's go, David. We can't let him get away!" she managed to yell out.

He holstered his weapon and removed his knife from his belt. Then, after cutting a long slender branch from a papyrus tree, he waded out into the river.

"Grab hold, Anali."

She took hold of the branch as she went by and held on tight. He landed her like a fisherman would a trout, and pulled her up out of the water.

"You'll never make it, Anali. Not with that bag."

She sat there with mud caked on her bare legs and water dripping from her nose.

"Anali, I think we should go back upstream and see if we can find a boat. Even if you had managed to swim across you would be five miles downriver."

"But, David we won't know which way they went."

"If we can get across the river and find where they came ashore we'll find them."

"Then we had better get moving," she said getting to her feet.

"Where are your shoes?"

"Oh wait," she said, fishing through her bag.

They moved south upriver, disturbing the wildlife as they ran along the riverbank. The crocodiles scurried to get into the water, the birds took to the air, and they gave a small herd of sleeping hippos a wide berth. When they reached the spot where Anali had first spotted the terrorists, they found a local fishermen lying face down in the mud. It looked as though his throat had been cut from ear to ear, and his lifeless body was already attracting scavengers.

They continued on for another mile before they came upon two local fishermen, but no boat. However, they did learn from the men that there was a small village on the river less than four kilometers further up.

They had covered the first two of the four kilometers when Anali stopped and gazed out across the water, and then up in the sky to find the sun. With sorrow in her soft voice she said,

"I fear, David, that the son-of-a-dog will not find his way to his evil God today. It will be dark soon."

"I'm sure you're right, Anali," he sadly agreed. "Our only chance now is to wait for him to make his move at the Peace Talks."

When they made the decision to turn back, they were over four miles from where they left the Saab, and the sun was setting fast. David led the way up and away from the river through the tall papyrus, and by the time they reached the sea of Nile river grass, the sun's light had all but faded out.

The darkness filled with the sound of flying insects, and the wings of bats soon joined the chorus. An uncountable number of stars began to show themselves, and within an hour, the moon released only half its brilliance to light up the heavens. A wild pig squealed and scurried from their path; then a cobra raised its head above the grass and flexed its hood to warn them off.

"Big snake," David said.

"That's a king cobra, David. I have heard that they are very rarely seen anymore in Egypt."

"Not rarely enough, Anali," he said while pulling his weapon and activating the laser.

"Don't shoot it, David."

He pointed the red beam and painted the snakes eyes. The cobra quickly reacted and dropped its head, then slithered off through the tall grass.

"I really don't like snakes," he said before continuing on.

"Did you know that the ancient Egyptians believed that the cobra was both the protector of the kings, and a demon of the underworld?"

"I would have to agree with them on the demon part."

They found the highway and decided the car was somewhere to the north.

Chapter 6

Long before the Sahara sand collected the morning
light, the Saab was back on the road and, after two and a
half hours, they were closing in fast on the capital city of
Cairo. David was behind the wheel and Anali had fallen
asleep in the passenger seat beside him after spending
two hours giving him a history lesson on Egypt, and the
capital city that now lay just minutes ahead.

The Nile River Basin lay between mountains of
sand and, not withstanding the Mediterranean coast, was
the only source of life in all of Egypt. Its blue life-giving
water found its way north out of the depths of Africa,
feeding the abundant plant life and the Egyptian people
since the very beginning of time.

Cairo, according to Anali, was the most populated
city in Africa. In 1805, Mohamed Ali of Egypt named Cairo
as the capital of his independent empire.

The city is located on the banks and islands of the
Nile in the northern part of Egypt, where the river leaves
the desert bound valley. There, the river spreads out into
two wide branches, and forms what is called the Nile Delta
Region.

Most of Egypt's history was centered in and around
Cairo. The Great Pyramid of Giza, the Necropolis of
Memphis, the Sphinx, and many more ancient wonders
dating back to the sixth century were all centered in Cairo.
The lights of the city that never slept marked the night sky
with a glowing shroud, and the well-lit widows of the many
high rises along the river shimmered across the water's
darkened surface.

The narrow, sand-covered road ended, and a
modern four-lane highway just seemed to appear out of
nowhere. It was exactly three am according to the clock

embedded in the dashboard, and yet the city was already alive with activity. It was the morning of the fourteenth, and delegations from all over the Middle East were either on their way or had already touched down.

Anali flinched when David gently touched her arm to wake her, but when she opened her eyes she knew why he had cut short her dreams.

"We're here, Anali. Where do we need to go?"

"Do you see the car lights going over the river? Take that bridge across to Greater Cairo. That is where the government offices and most of the fine hotels are located."

"We will need to fuel up soon," he said, pointing to the gauge.

"There will be a petrol stop before you reach the bridge," she assured him.

They were both hungry, tired, and very thirsty when they finally pulled off and stopped for fuel. It had been a long day. In their haste to get to the dock that morning they had no time to eat, nor had they given any thought to taking any water along. The last drink of fresh water either of them had was from the muddy bank of the Nile, five hours earlier.

David stood by at the pump with the attendant while Anali ran inside for a six-pack of bottled water to drink and, as she put it, to freshen up. When she returned from the small convenience store, she took to the driver's seat. She drove across the long expansion bridge and turned left down a wide, well lit parkway. She slowed down as she passed two twin towers on the waterfront, which, although much shorter, resembled the two in New York City that no longer stood. Beyond the twin Al Ashly bank buildings was the Ramses Hilton Hotel that was almost as tall.

"I stayed here once when I came to the city," Anali explained as she turned into the parking lot. The Ramses Hilton Hotel had a modern flavor and was an architectural masterpiece. Its thirty-six stories came very close to rivaling the neighboring Al Ashly Towers.

Anali pulled in under the hotel's expansive breezeway that accommodated four lanes of traffic, and stopped across from the huge lobby. It was three-thirty am, and the parking attendants were hustling to handle the patronage both coming and going from the busy Hilton. David stepped out into the humid early morning air with both of their bags in hand and waited while Anali turned her keys over to a young Egyptian lad wearing a bright red jacket, matching pants, and a Fez. When she had her parking stub in hand, she circled behind her Saab as it pulled away from the curb.

"I hope the Major General won't mind if we spend some of his money," she said with a smile as she took her bag from David's hand.

"Tonight's on David Dupia, Anali," he said, patting the pocket containing his wallet.

The tinted glass doors parted automatically and the cool refrigerated air welcomed them to the lobby. They walked over to one of many windows marked 'Check In', and were greeted by an older woman dressed in the hotel's signature red jacket, floor length red skirt, and traditional headscarf.

"Can I help you, Sir," she asked, first in Arabic, and then, before waiting for a response, repeated her question in broken English.

"We would like a room," Anali responded.

"How will you be paying, Sir," the woman asked, looking directly at David and ignoring Anali.

David opened his wallet and held out his Visa card.

"With plastic, ma'am."

The woman looked over the counter and scanned first Anali and then David from head to toe. Their shoes were muddy, their clothes dirty, and they both had grass and twigs in their hair. Then, with a look that said maybe you should go elsewhere, she said,

"Our least expensive accommodations are three hundred dollars a night, Sir. Maybe..." Anali interrupted her and, in a condescending tone, asked,

"How much are your *better* accommodations?" The woman's expression changed, and so did her tone. She smiled at Anali this time and replied,

"Our suites range from five hundred to six thousand. What would you prefer?"

"Give us something in the middle," Anali said in a tone that suggested to David that she wanted to pull the snooty clerk over the counter.

David broke in and suggested,

"Why don't we have a look at something in the five hundred range. If it's not to our liking, we'll let you know."

"Very well, Sir," the woman said, as she swiped his card through her machine.

"Your room is number 3444. Take one of the elevators to the thirty-fourth floor," she explained, pointing across the lobby. She handed two key cards to David and said,

"If you should require room service or anything else at all, there is a directory in the suite." David accepted the cards, thanked the female clerk, and turned to Anali,

"Shall we go up and see if the room is adequate, Anali?"

Two men and a woman stepped out of the elevator just as David and Anali reached the doors. Anali explained, after they had stepped inside and the doors closed, that the men were Saudi's. It was obvious to David and Anali from the woman's red uniform, that she worked for the hotel.

The elevator started up slowly with a jerk, and then seemed to smooth out as it picked up speed, and the rest of the ride was smooth and non-stop to their designated floor.

Small sconce lights marked the position of the doorways up and down the long hallway and, according to the numbers on the wall; and the direction the camel's nose was pointing, Room 3444 was to their left.

David handed the key cards to Anali before they walked out of the elevator and she led the way down the long hallway. The small, green light flashed, indicating she had access, and the solid core door opened inward.

On the left was the door to the bathroom. Inside, on the exterior wall was a long counter top with double sinks. On the opposing wall a large tub/shower combination, and hidden behind the open door was the water closet. All the fixtures were white in color, and the floor tile matched the Sahara sands.

Just before the short hallway ended and the bedroom began, there was a small open closet with un-attachable hangers for them to hang up their extra clothes, if they had thought to bring any along.

The king size bed was on the left side of the room between two end tables. Anali stopped and set her bag down on a much larger matching dresser that adorned the opposing wall across from the foot of the bed.

Beyond the bedroom, straight away through an arch, the exterior wall was all glass. The drapes and sheers were drawn back, exposing the night sky.

A round maple wood table, surrounded by straight backed, mock-leather chairs filled the center of the room, with a matching couch, two easy chairs and a television completing the décor of the sitting room.

David dropped his bag on the couch before walking over and opening the French doors leading out onto the balcony. Left of the doors was another table and two more chairs, and to his right was a covered hot tub. He looked down on the Nile and then out over the city.

"Anali, come have a look."

"I will look after I have had a shower, David," she said as she was disappearing into the bathroom.

He walked over to the small television, turned it on and found CNN International before returning to the couch.

In the time it took Anali to shower, he learned from a bunch of Arabs speaking gibberish that the Peace Talks would start at ten the next morning. Then he watched live coverage of various protests that were being carried out throughout the Middle East.

Ivan Wikert

When Anali came out of the bathroom into the hallway, she was wearing a white bathrobe with the Hilton's emblem embroidered in red over her heart. She made her way across the room and stopped at the windows, still working feverishly to dry her freshly washed hair.

"The bathroom is all yours, David. There is another one of these folded on the counter," she explained, shaking her collar so he knew to what she was referring.

David disappeared into the bathroom and she immediately heard the water running. She had just turned off the noise coming from the tube, and was headed for the balcony when the phone next to the bed rang. She turned and walked slowly to the bedside, apprehensive about answering the persistent house phone, but after the fifth ring, she brought the receiver to her ear. She listened but remained silent.

"Is that you David, my boy," a very familiar voice asked.

"No, father, it is Anali."

"Oh, good. How are you, my dear?"

"How did you know we were here?"

"A flag came up on our computer. David's credit card. You know how it works. Is he there with you?"

"Yes, father, he is. He is in the shower, though."

"Has he been helpful to you?"

"Very much so. He makes it all look so easy."

"I am glad to hear that my gamble is paying off."

"My brother has learned very well how to resolve problems."

"We are just finding that out, Anali. He apparently resolved a few problems on his way to Tel Aviv."

"David told me what happened in Tyre."

"The Lebanese government is up in arms. They're blaming Israel."

"What's new, father?"

"You're right, my dear. Did you get the bird you were expecting?"

65

"No, Sir, but if it shows up here we will."

"I had hoped that you would have received the package in Alexandria."

"It arrived there but was rerouted to Cairo. We almost intercepted it en route but it slipped through our fingers. I believe it has been delayed and possibly damaged, so it may not arrive at all."

"Well, stay on it my dear. Stay in Cairo until your uncle leaves town. I have already explained to him that you are close by."

"Thank you, father. I hope to see you soon."

The phone went dead and Anali returned the receiver to the cradle just as the bathroom door opened and spread light into the dimly lit room.

"The Major General called while you were showering, David," she said before he had time to exit the hall.

"Really? How did he know we were here?"

"Credit card."

"Oh. Did you tell him we lost that damn bird?"

"Yes I did."

"And what did he say?"

"That we should remain here until we get him, or the Peace Talks are over and the Prime Minister is safely back in Tel Aviv. Also, he said he alerted the Secret Police to our presence."

David looked over at the clock on the night stand and said,

"It's 4:15. Why don't you call down and order us some breakfast," he asked, deferring any further comment on her conversation with Sol Kline.

"What would you like for breakfast, David?"

"Anything, as long as it comes with eggs, meat, and coffee if they have it."

She placed her order for a fruit plate, toast, and goat's milk, and requested steak and eggs, and a pot of English coffee. Then she said,

"Charge it to Room 3444, and add no more than

twenty percent."

"The Major General said that the Lebanese government is blaming Israel for those *problems* you resolved when you were in Lebanon."

"What was he referring to?"

"Well, by resolved he meant killed. Hezbollah and Hamas are what we call problems."

"Oh."

She smiled at him and said,

"I'm looking forward to resolving many more problems, David."

Forty minutes came and went before a knock at the door told them breakfast was served. They sat down at the table looking out over the skyline and watched the morning begin to awaken.

"Anali, I think I am going to try and get an hour or two of sleep."

Without saying another word, she got up from the table, walked around the foot of the bed, turned off the light, dropped the robe to the floor and crawled into bed. David set the alarm for 9:00 am and stretched out on the window side of the oversize bed.

Chapter 7

After swimming the crocodile-infested Nile, Ahmed, Askari, and Rashad made their way south in search of another conveyance. The Falcon was fuming, and with every step became more and more obsessed. On one hand he knew that killing the Israeli Prime Minster was his top priority, but on the other hand he wanted to avenge the death of his son.

His first-born son, Seleh was dead at the hands of the Infidels who had chased them from Alexandria. From the muddy riverbank, he had watched helplessly as his son drifted with the Nile's rolling current while clinging to the overturned skiff. He felt sorrow and pain when the boy's life slipped away and his body melted into the depths, and he cursed the man and woman who stood watching from the far shoreline. He swore to Allah that he would avenge what happened this day.

When they were forced to bail out of the boat to avoid the Infidel's bullets, they lost all but one of their firearms and most of their ammunition. Only Askari had managed to hold onto his weapon and the full clip inside. If Ahmed wanted revenge, it would have to wait until after they found a fresh supply of weapons.

That night, just as the sun was about to set in the western sky, Ahmed, Askari, and Rashad walked into a small village just four kilometers upriver from where they had climbed out of the water. They were tired, hungry, and had been feeding the mosquitoes for hours.

The fifteen small houses were spread out along the riverbank in the shade of large date palm trees. All the structures were small and had been built out of mud brick with wooden thatched roofs. There was no electricity or running water, and no sign of any vehicles. There were no roads, and the only way in or out of the remote fishing community was by boat or on foot. There were twenty-five villagers, and over half of them were children under the age of twelve. All of the men made their living from fishing. They all were followers of Islam, and seemed sympathetic to their visitors' cause. The men found refuge for the night in a typical ancient Egyptian kitchen where there was no ceiling overhead. They broke bread with a young man named Ayham, and a large Sudanese man named Hamza, who worked with him. Ayham owned a twenty-one foot open bowed powerboat that he and his Sudanese friend used to make their living, so when Ahmed offered them a thousand dollars to take him and his friends to Cairo, he readily agreed.

The sun was just beginning to shed light on the Nile River Basin. Ahmed, Askari, and a very reluctant Rashad sat quietly as the twenty-one foot powerboat they were riding in made its way upriver. Blue smoke boiled up behind the stern, and white foam pushed out from the struggling props. Crocodiles began to leave the cool of the river in search of the sun's warmth, and birds of all shapes, sizes and colors took to the wing as the boat passed by. Ayham was keeping his keen eyes on the surface of the river to avoid the larger floating debris. Ahmed was sitting near the stern looking back downstream. His thoughts were of his oldest child who he would never see again, and the woman at home who was yet to grieve.

The two Infidels were still at the top of his priority list but, like his pursuers, he realized he would not find them on the river. Askari had convinced him sometime late in the night that the two responsible for his son's death had to have somehow found out about their plan to assassinate the Prime Minister of Israel, and would most likely go to Cairo. He reasoned that even though the Infidels knew about the plot, they could not knew about the stinger missile or the old abandoned Church.

"I swear to you, Ahmed, I will help you find them after we do this thing."

Askari's thoughts were with the brown leather case full of cash that he watched float away on the current, and the man and woman from hell who had caused the loss. Who were they? How did they find out the Falcon was going to Egypt?

Rashad's arm was hurting more this morning than it had the day before. He wanted nothing more than to find his way to a doctor. His thoughts were the same as they had been from the moment the first shot rang out. Why did he get into the car with Ahmed? He should have stayed behind with his woman. Hell, he could have already had his wound cared for in Alexandria.

Ayham was only twenty-five years old, and unmarried. He was five foot eleven inches tall, and one hundred sixty pounds. Like many Egyptians, he shaved his head and wore a Fez, but found the Galabya impractical for work on the river. He preferred cargo pants and a white cotton shirt. He knew the river like the back of his hand and, because he marketed his fish there, knew the city of Cairo well. However, when questioned about the old Church he said he had no knowledge of it. Ayham could not care less if the Israeli Prime Minister lived or died. All he was interested in was the money that Ahmed had promised him.

Hamza sat alone up in the bow. He was a big, dark skinned converted Muslim from the city of Abri in Sudan. He was over six foot six inches tall, and very muscular. His dress was more Sudanese, with canvas boots laced half the way up to his knees, white canvas pants, and a vest-like shirt open on the sides and in the front. He said that when he converted to Islam he had changed his name to Hamza, and that he found the name in the Koran. His reasoning for volunteering was simply stated as hatred for Jews. He said that he had never seen one, but the good book declares them enemies of Islam and, of course, he also could use the money that Ahmed had promised him

for getting them to Cairo. The stage was now set for the
Syrian-born plot to unfold.

Chapter 8

David opened his eyes just as the alarm clock clicked to summon in a local radio station. Anali was lying on the bed in a fetal position, with her back turned toward him. Her head moved when she heard the alarm and she moaned,

"I am not ready to wake up."

"It's 9:02, Anali. We should get ready to go to the Peace Talks," he said as he rolled from the bed.

She sat up, exposing her bare back, and looked around the room for just a minute before bending over to retrieve her robe from the floor where she had discarded it three hours earlier. After slipping it around her shoulders, she got to her feet and shuffled off in the direction of the bathroom.

David dressed quickly after she had left the room, and just as 9:05 rolled into view on the clock, they were both dressed and out the door.

"Do you believe the Falcon will show up at the talks," she asked, as the elevator doors closed.

"I wouldn't bet on it right now, but you never know. Maybe we'll get lucky."

The morning was already showing signs that another steaming hot day was on the way when they walked out of the hotel into the open air. Anali handed her parking stub to the attendant, and while they waited for the young Egyptian to retrieve the Saab, two long, black limousines were filling up with dignitaries.

David handed a Canadian five-dollar bill to the attendant before joining Anali inside the Saab. She pushed the lever forward to claim low gear and they fell in behind the two stretch limos full of *Rag Head's*, as Anali referred to the Saudi's

72

They circled around, following the parkway, and drove up onto the bridge heading east across the river to Giza. They followed closely behind the limousines until they turned into the University. There was already a long line of vehicles ahead of them, and the whole precession came to an abrupt stop.

Anali opened her door and removed herself from the car. She walked around the front of the Saab to the curb, and then quickly returned to the driver's seat.

"The Egyptian police are searching the vehicles before allowing them to enter the campus parking area. I do not see any Israeli Security anywhere. We will never get past the checkpoint, David. We will have to park outside and walk in unarmed," she suggested.

David looked back over his shoulder at the line of vehicles that had already pulled in behind them and said,

"Okay, as soon as you get the chance, pull out of line and let's get out of here."

She did just that with out any hesitation. The small two door Saab's front end bounced when the front wheels went up on the center divider and the rear tires squealed when she put her foot to the floor.

"How was that," she asked, grinning from ear to ear.

David looked back over his shoulder again to see if they had drawn the attention of the Egyptian Security, just as she turned right onto the main road. But then, before he had time to turn his attention forward again, the Saab swerved and came to a stop at the curb between a green van and another small white sports car.

"You know, David, I don't believe the Falcon will try for the Prime Minister here. There's too much security. If he tries anything now, it will be on the road between here and the airport."

"Well, maybe you should walk inside and inform your people that you are here and that you're going to be following them when they leave."

"Why don't you come with me?"

73

"Because I am not really here, remember. "

"What will you do after this, David Stone?"

He was silent for a time because he had not given any thought to a life after this. When he went into the water three days earlier, he fully expected he would not live to see another sunrise. However, here he was sitting in a white Saab next to a very pretty Mossad Agent in the land of the Pharaoh's.

"I don't know, Anali. I will have to give '*after this*' a little more thought."

"Well, David, you give '*after this*' some thought while I go find Israeli Security."

She opened the door and slid out of the Saab, then walked away across the small grass-covered park toward the gates. She did not look back.

Watching her walk away, it was hard for David to imagine she was a Major in the Mossad, but he knew that she was. In what little time he had spent with her, he found Anali to be like no woman he had ever known. She was, by all accounts, very well educated, yet very down to earth. She was every inch a woman, yet when the lead began to fly and the chips were down, she reacted better than some men he had known. She was Canadian and Indian and chose to put her life on the line for a small country to which she had no ties.

The morning sun had already found its place above the palm trees, and through the glass inside the confines of the two passenger Saab, it was sweltering. David opened the passenger side door, slid out into the open air, and walked over to the small grass-covered park. From where he stood, he could see the tall, white columns and ornate iron gates that greeted students, faculty and visitors to the ultramodern University of Cairo.

Palm trees lined the stone walkways leading up to the gate where Anali now stood arguing with three uniformed Egyptian policemen. David moved closer, but not too close, and found a shaded bench at the edge of the small well-manicured park and sat down. He watched as one of the uniformed men backed away and disappeared behind one of the two large, white columns. The two remaining security guards stood with arms folded across their chests between Anali and the gates. David was too far away to hear what was being said, but from the gestures she was making with her arms, he could tell she was giving them a piece of her mind.

The third man, who had disappeared, soon reappeared, and opened one of the large, ornate, arched iron gates. There was a brief discussion and then he escorted Anali inside.

When David could no longer see her, he turned his attention to the building that lay protected behind the polished limestone walls. It was three stories high, with massive white stone pillars all long the front. The roof resembled the white house over the doorways, and there was a golden dome on the right side of center. Beyond the buildings wide expanse, was a four-sided clock tower, tall enough that it could be seen from anywhere on campus.

David's eyes picked up movement in the clock tower, and again on the roof of the building above the main entrance. Overall, he counted twenty well-armed Sentries holding the high ground.

He decided immediately that Anali was right. If the Falcon still had designs on the Head of State, there was no way that he could pull it off here. He sat back, spread his arms out on the back of the wrought iron bench and watched the people as they passed by.

Chapter 9

Twenty-five miles away, on the far west side of Cairo where the river divided to form the Nile Delta and the city of Cairo began, the Falcon and his fellow terrorists put ashore.

The Peace Talks were just getting underway, and Ahmed knew that they were being held across the river at the University. He, himself had never been to the city. He had a good idea from the map he had left in Tyre where the airport was, but the man he was depending on for the location of the old Church was dead. He questioned Rashad about the old Church and, although he had been to Cairo International several times, he had never heard about or seen any old, abandoned Catholic Church.

The Infidels had put him way behind schedule. Now he had only until six O'clock tomorrow evening to find Zaabi's people and the American-made stinger missile left over from the Afghanistan war with the Russians, get back across the river, and find the old Church.

His dead friend had explained that about a half mile from the river, in the middle of the Muslim section of Cairo near the Muhammad Ali of Egypt Mosque, he would find the machine shop where Al Zaabi's brother worked.

Ayham had assured him that he knew where the Mosque was, and docked his watercraft in a small secluded cove where a dozen or more fishing boats were moored.

It was early afternoon and the African sun was punishing mother earth with its intense heat.

Old Cairo was much the same as it had been in the days of the Pharaohs, with streets paved with cobblestone embedded in the sands of time. The houses were, for the most part, mud brick and thatching like those where Ayham lived upriver. The men and woman dressed alike in white linen Galabyas, and most of the children wore nothing at all.

The locals eyes followed the five strangers as they walked slowly through the streets. Ayham led the way, scattering sheep, goats, and an occasional small child from underfoot. It wasn't long before they could see the twin towers and dome of the Mosque that stood high above the city streets.

They walked close to a half a mile through the narrow streets before the first vehicle came into view and pavement replaced the cobblestones beneath their feet. The structures became larger and more modern, and the streets much busier.

There was a crowded outdoor market and other places of business surrounding the Mosque. Al Zaabi had mentioned many times that his family lived near the business district that surrounds the holy place, and that his brother worked in one of many machine shops in the district.

"We shall split up and find the machine shop where Al Zaabi Hussan's brother works. We will meet back here at the market in one hour," Ahmed instructed.

Ayham and Mamza turned south, inquiring at each shop along the way about Ali Hussan. Askari went north on his own, and Rashad followed Ahmed across the wide thoroughfare to the Mosque.

When Ahmed went inside and the others were out of sight, Rashad saw his opportunity to get away and go in search of a doctor. He walked back to the street, and when he noticed a taxi coming his way, he held up his good arm to flag it down.

"I need you to take me to a hospital," he instructed, after sliding into the back seat. It wasn't until the small green and white English ford pulled away from the curb, and Rashad looked back to make sure that no one saw him, that he relaxed, sighed with relief, and closed his eyes.

Chapter 10

David was engrossed in watching a half dozen young Egyptian men playing soccer in the park when he heard Anali's voice.

"Why aren't you playing, David?"

He stood up and turned around to see her standing just a few feet away.

"It's too hot, and it's the wrong kind of football for a Yank." She laughed and closed the distance between them.

"I just came from talking with the head of Israeli Security. He informed me that the Prime Minister is not leaving Cairo until six tomorrow evening. He said that they will be here at the University until late tonight and that they will be staying on board the plane inside the hangar at Cairo International. They will then leave the airport no latter than 8:00 am, and come back for another round of talks starting at nine. I gave them a description of my Saab and said I would be following them."

"And what was his response?"

"He said, *whatever.*"

"That's it? Just, whatever?"

"No, David, then he invited me to stay with him at the hangar tonight, the low-life pig."

"What did you say?"

"I said, you are a low life pig and if I were a member of your team I would bring you up on charges."

"And?"

"Oh, he just laughed and said, *whatever,* again."

"Well, it sounds to me like they're not overly concerned, so why don't you and I go back to the hotel and have some lunch and get a little rest. We'll come back after eight tonight."

"Sounds good to me, David." Anali started the Saab, made one of her trademark U-turns in the street, and headed back toward the hotel.

The traffic was heavy when they turned onto the bridge, and became even heavier when she turned off on the parkway. They were less than a mile from the Hilton when they both noticed a woman carrying a small boy in her arms, and as they passed by David noticed that the boy seemed limp. The woman had a panicked look on her face and was walking very fast along the side of the road.

"Stop the car, Anali!" Without questioning why, she pulled to the curb and stopped.

"Back up. I think there's something wrong." Anali put the Saab in reverse, backed up to where the woman was, then stopped again. David stepped out onto the curb to the sound of the wailing woman's voice.

"My son has been hurt. He needs a doctor!"

David turned to the still wide-open car door and told the woman to get in.

"You take her and the child, Anali. I'll hail a cab and follow you."

David closed the door after the woman was in the seat and watched the Saab speed away into traffic. He immediately started walking backwards, looking over the oncoming traffic for a taxi. Anali wasn't even out of sight before an old pickup truck pulled over and rolled up beside him.

A spot here and there suggested that the old truck had been green in another lifetime, but now it was mostly the color of rust. In the back, inside the chicken-wire covered racks was a full load of brown and white spotted goats.

"Where is it you wish to go, my friend," an old man in a full white beard asked.

"To the nearest hospital," David answered in Arabic.

"Please get in. I can take you there."

"David opened the door and sat down on a burlap sack that protected the bare springs. The old man put the truck in gear and they were off, leaving a cloud of black smoke behind them.

"What brings you to Al-Qahira?"

"Al-Qahira?"

"Some call this place Cairo, but it is Al-Qahira to others."

"I am here sightseeing with my sister."

"Is it she that you go to the hospital to see?"

"No, she is giving an injured child and his mother a ride to the hospital. Her car was too small for everyone, so I stayed behind."

The words had just left his lips when the old truck sputtered and rocked to one side, then bounced as it hit a speed bump and came to a squeaky stop in front of the hospital. Anali's Saab was at the curb out front with the passenger side door still standing wide open. David could see her standing near the entrance.

The old man smiled and said,

"May your God protect you, my friend."

David opened the door and stepped out with the burlap sack still clinging to the seat of his pants. He opened his wallet and extracted a twenty-dollar bill and handed it to the old man, and pushed the sack back inside the cab.

"Thank you, Sir. You are a Good Samaritan."

The old man looked at David and smiled again.

"The Good Samaritan is in the book of the Infidels, my friend. You would be wise not to give yourself away."

David thanked him again and then tried to outrun the black smoke as the old truck bucked and sputtered when it pulled away from the curb.

"I like the taxi you picked, David," Anali said as he walked up to the hospital doors."

"It got me here, funny girl. How is the boy?"

"Not good."

"Let's go inside and check on him before we go," he said while pushing the door open.

There were four other women sitting in the waiting

room, but the boy and his mother were nowhere to be seen. Anali walked over to the front desk and inquired about the young boy. When she returned to where David was waiting, she said that he was with the doctor.

David and Anali were just about to turn around and leave when a tall, slender man dressed in a Galabya with his right arm in a sling came out of the infirmary. Anali immediately recognized Rashad from the courtyard on the outskirts of Alexandria. She grabbed David's right arm.

"That's one of the Falcon's men. He was the one driving the Toyota, David," she exclaimed, quickly slipping her hand inside her bag.

Rashad was walking straight toward David and Anali, but when he noticed the two of them staring at him he stopped dead in his tracks. Rashad knew that he had been made when he heard Anali say,

"He was the one driving the Toyota, David." He raised his good arm slowly over his head, and the look on his face said, *you got me.*

David looked Rashad over from head to foot and after seeing what Anali saw, raised his right hand and with his index finger made a gesture that commanded Rashad to come closer.

"I am only the driver. I never meant you any harm," the cornered man exclaimed.

"Where is your friend, Ahmed," Anali asked. She had already armed her nine millimeter, but had not removed it from her bag.

"When last I saw him he was in the Muslim quarter, near the Mosque of Mohammed Ali."

"What's your name?"

"Rashad Attar."

"Well, Rashad I think we should take a walk," David said, taking him by the arm with the sling. They walked out of the hospital together, with Rashad in front, and turned left across the lawn. They came to a secluded bench that was marked "Bus Stop" in Arabic, English, and French where David ordered Rashad to sit down. Anali sat down on the other end of the bench and produced her blue steel automatic from her bag.

"Tell us everything you know about the Falcon's plan to assassinate the Israeli Prime Minister."

"I told you, I am just the one who was hired to drive him to Cairo. I know very little."

"If that is all you can tell us I will put you down right here," she said; and from her tone, he knew she meant it.

"I can tell you that he is in the old city to find the brother of the man you killed when we drove away from Alexandria. I heard Ahmed say that Al Zaabi's brother is holding a stinger missile for him."

"Did you hear anything about where he is planning to use the stinger," David asked.

"Somewhere north of the airport, near the river. He questioned me about an old Catholic Church."

"Do you know where it is?"

"No, but it must be close to the airport. He said you could see the terminal from the roof."

"Did you hear anything about how they're planning to get to the Church?"

"They have a boat now, and two more men with them. Ahmed cursed you and swore he would have revenge against you both." That remark got a laugh out of Anali.

Without provocation, he went on to explain that Ahmed's son was the one that died in the river, and that the money, all one million dollars of it, went under with the boy. Then he explained all that he knew about Ayham and the Sudanese man, Hamza, who were now helping the Falcon.

"You mentioned your employer; what is his roll in all this?"

"He put up the money."

"Just him, or are others involved?"

"I only know that he is involved."

"What is his name, Anali questioned.

"Abdul Salam al-Walid."

83

"Where is he now?"

"He is most likely here in Cairo. He is the Syrian Ambassador."

"Well, I think we might just let you live, Rashad Attar, but we can't let you go until this is all over. We wouldn't want you running back into the old city and warning Ahmed."

"I ran away from him. If he sees me again, I am sure that he will kill me."

"Well, you are going with us to the airport, and you will be the guest of the Israeli's until this is over."

"The doctors say that I must have medicine or the infection in my arm will kill me," he said, holding out a handwritten prescription.

"Fine, we will stop somewhere and get you your meds, but then you're off to a holding cell."

"It would be cheaper and far less trouble if we just shot him here and threw his carcass in the river," Anali argued.

"Please, I have a wife and children who need me!" he pleaded.

"Well, Rashad, if you continue to cooperate we promise to let you go home when this is all over. Don't we Anali?" She looked at David and smiled.

"All right, David. But we don't have room for him in the Saab."

"I will hail a taxi and take Rashad with me to the airport. You can follow us in the Saab."

David took Rashad by the arm again and they walked to the busy street in front of the hospital.

It was not long before a taxi answered his wave, and when David and his captive got into the cab, Anali slipped behind the wheel of her vehicle.

The driver of the cab explained that Cairo International was fifteen kilometers north of the city on the west side of the Nile and said it would take twenty to thirty minutes to get there. They made one stop to fill Rashad's prescription and then headed for Cairo International.

Ivan Wikert

While the road passed under the wheels of the Cairo taxi, Rashad became more at ease. He began to talk more about Ahmed and the ill-fated mission to assassinate Israel's top dog. He told David that the money was hand carried to Alexandria by a courier for the Syrian Ambassador and that, because he and his wife were the caretakers of the Ambassador's vacation home, he was ordered to meet the Falcon and his men. He said that he was ordered by his boss to see that the money and weapons were delivered, and again swore that he was not a terrorist.

"Why then did you drive them out of the compound, Rashad?"

"I have asked myself many times that same question, Sir. I can only say that the Falcon is said to be blessed by Allah, and I fear him."

"Blessed or not, Rashad, I have come a long way to kill him, and not even your Allah will stop me."

Rashad looked at the man in the seat beside him and thought back to that day when the American stepped out in front of the gates and fired two shots, killing one on the roof and wounding him as he ran for cover. Then he thought about what happened at the river.

"I believe you will, Sir," he said looking forward out the window at the hills of desert sand and houses.

The meter up front on the dashboard continued to track the miles, converting them into denars, and the sands of time seemed to stretch as far as the eye could see out the driver's side of the car, but on the right, houses sat side by side in the greenery that the Nile River provided. It was quiet for a full ten minutes, and then the haggard Rashad asked,

"If you please, Sir, who sent you to kill Ahmed?"

David thought about it for a full ten seconds and then for lack of a better answer he said,

"I was sent by the first born son of the King of the Jews, and my name is also David."

Rashad again looked away, this time at the dark

eyes staring back at him in the rear view mirror. The Egyptian driver, who was a Muslim, had been listening to his passengers and found their conversation very interesting. He had listened in on many conversations concerning the man known as the Falcon, who was spoken of often in the streets and mosques throughout Cairo.

The way he figured it, the Falcon was a holy warrior, and in the back seat of his taxi was a man who had come to kill an icon. He looked into the eyes of Rashad in the mirror and saw a traitor to Islam. At his side in the front seat, hidden under a towel, was an old British-made revolver that he carried for protection from those who would try to rob him. He raised his right hand to the mirror and turned it just enough so that he could see David's face and then returned his hand to the steering wheel.

Just then, from somewhere high overhead in the haze of urban industrial pollution, the high-pitched whine of a jet's engines penetrated the steel and glass of the taxi.

The driver slowed down and pulled off the road, turned and looked at the two men in the back seat and said,

"I feel something is wrong with my taxi. Please stay inside. I will check it out."

The short, heavy-set Egyptian opened the door and stepped out. He disappeared from sight when he bent down near the front of the car, and when he reappeared he started walking along the driver's side toward the back.

"Did you hear anything that would make you think there was a problem with this vehicle," David asked after removing his weapon from his belt.

"No, I heard nothing strange."

"Well, Rashad, duck your head down when I open the door." David kicked his door open and rolled out on the ground and Rashad buried his head between his knees. A loud, single gunshot pierced the silence just as David hit the ground and came up with his automatic trained on the cab driver. The Egyptian was standing near the trunk lid.

His face was racked with a painful expression, and his
eyes were open beyond wide. His revolver was still tightly
gripped in his right hand, hanging straight down with the
business end pointed at the ground.

David had his small caliber automatic leveled and
was just about to fire when the Egyptian let the British
revolver slip from his hand. The weapon landed barrel first
in the sand and the man slumped down to his knees. His
eyes closed, his body wilted to the ground, and he gasped
his last breath.

It was not until the threat lay dead at his feet that
David noticed Anali. She was standing between the cab
and the open door of the Saab fifteen feet away, with her
nine millimeter at arm's length. She slowly lowered her
weapon and said,

"That man was going to shoot you!"

"I can see that. Good thing for me you were behind
us."

"She smiled and acted is if she was blowing smoke
from her gun's barrel, then smiled,

"You owe me one, David Stone."

About that time, Anali's eyes looked beyond David
and focused on a green sedan that had appeared out of
nowhere. It was coming from the direction of the airport at
a high rate of speed. There was no time to cover up what
had just taken place. As the vehicle passed by it slowed
down and the driver and both passengers stared back on
the scene. The sedan picked up speed and David and
Anali watched it drive off.

"I think we should get out of here, Anali. Come help
me put this back shooter in the trunk before anyone else
comes this way."

She took the dead taxi driver by the feet, and he
lifted the torso. On the count of three, they threw the
dumpy little man in with the spare tire and closed the lid.

Rashad opened his door and stepped out, letting
his door close under its own weight.

"I am a good driver, David. Let me drive us the rest

87

of the way."

"Sure, Rashad, get in behind the wheel."

"I guess you and that terrorist are now on a first name ..."

David cut her statement short when he pulled her close and kissed her the way she did him at the airport in Alexandria.

"I owe you my life, Anali Dupia," he said after he finally released his hold on her. She smiled at him, and winked.

"I will be right behind you," she said before turning and walking back to the Saab.

David slipped into the front seat this time and Rashad pulled the taxi back onto the road. He had witnessed more gun play and death in the last forty-eight hours than he had in all his forty-three years.

"If you can see your way clear to spare me Allah, I will forever be in your debt," he said to himself.

It was quiet inside the Cairo cab for the next three miles. David put his right arm on the back of the seat, reached forward and turned off the meter on the dashboard, then relaxed and watched the never-changing landscape.

After just a few short minutes had passed, the tops of the terminal buildings and the control tower came into view. The terminal's acre of glass shined like a gigantic mirror in the hot African sun. The complex was made up of two terminals connected together to form a right angle, with the control tower standing high above, and behind. The three concrete runways stretched out across the desert sand, to the north from terminal one, to the west from terminal two, and the third to the northwest from the tower.

"Pull in and park the cab over there, Rashad," David ordered, pointing to an expansive lot that was half-full of dust-covered vehicles.

Anali followed the taxi until it pulled into an empty slot, but parked the Saab three parking lanes farther down.

They all three exited the vehicles at the same time and walked away toward the terminal. Once they were inside the massive glass structure, David pointed to a café and suggested that they grab a bite before turning their captive over to the Israeli's for safekeeping. Anali let a faint laugh slip from her lips.

"What's funny," David asked.

"Oh, sorry. I thought it was funny when you said turn him over to the Jews for safe keeping, that's all."

"Why is that, Anali? Don't you think he would be safe with your friends?" She stopped dead in her tracks.

"David, I don't have any friends in Israeli Security. I am Mossad, and those anal-retentive Police Officers do not like us spooks. I personally do not think much of them either. I laughed because Jews hate Arabs, and Arabs hate Jews. "

"Rashad is not Arab, Anali. He is an Egyptian."

"David, trust me, when we tell them why we want them to hold him, his being Egyptian will not gain him any sympathy from Israeli Intelligence."

"Well, let's feed him before we hand him over then."

"Suit yourself, David," she said as they continued toward the café.

When they reached the doorway leading into the café, Anali stopped and pointed to the restrooms.

"Order for me, would you, David?" She turned right without waiting for an answer, and he and his Egyptian captive continued straight on and into the eatery. They sat down facing each other, and David ordered goat meat and cheese on flat bread and ice tea for three.

Rashad thanked him for the meal and then asked,

"Is the one you call Anali your woman?"

David could not help but laugh aloud,

"No, Rashad. Anali is not my woman."

"She scares me." Again, David laughed aloud.

The food had been on the table for ten full minutes, and both men had all but finished their portions when Anali returned and sat down.

"The Prime Minister's plane is in a heavily guarded hangar at the north end of the complexes. We can go there after we eat," she explained as she picked at what he had ordered for her. She looked across the table at David and added,

"What I would give to sit down in a nice restaurant where goat wasn't on the menu."

David topped off all three glasses from the carafe in the middle of the table and was just about to lift his glass to his own lips when Anali slapped a plane ticket down on the table."

"What's that for," David asked.

"It's for your new friend," she explained in English.

David picked up the folder and examined the contents. It was a one-way ticket to Alexandria, and it was scheduled to depart in one hour and fifteen minutes. He looked at her and smiled, then held the boarding pass out toward Rashad.

"Why the change of heart, Anali?"

"Just give it to him and tell him to be gone before I change my mind."

"Rashad, we are letting you go. However, if we find out you tried to warn Ahmed, we will find you. Do you understand me?"

"Yes, Sir. I swear on my mother's grave that I will say nothing to anyone."

Rashad stood up and started to turn away but paused long enough to thank them both one more time. He walked slowly across the floor to a terminal gate then looked back at the man and woman who were still seated in the small airport café. When he saw them look in his direction, he raised his only good arm to his lips in a gesture of prayer, bowed ever so slightly, and turned to go through the passenger gate.

Anali retrieved her cell phone from her bag and made a call to the one man in Tel Aviv who had the Prime Minister's ear. She explained what they knew and how they knew it in the private little code that only the two of them shared, and then asked Major General Kline to call the Prime Minister and fill him in.

"Tell him that we are going to spend some more of his money, Anali," David said.

"David and I are going shopping for some clothes, and then after a good night's sleep and breakfast in the morning, we are going to find my bird, father."

"Just bring me that bird, my darling."

"We will. Goodbye, father," she said ending the conversation.

David and Anali spent the next hour sitting and talking more about his and her lives before they met, and what the future might hold for each. David asked her when the last time was she had gone home to Canada to see her family.

"I flew home two years ago for one month. My mother and *real* brother live in a suburb south of Montreal. Hampstead is near the airport where my mother works. She has a flower and gift shop inside the terminal."

"What does your brother do, Anali?"

"Halian is a doctor. He calls himself Hal. He is married and has three children."

"What about you, David? When was the last time you went home?"

"It's has been a long time, Anali; nearly six years."

"Why so long?"

"I guess because I've been over here. You know, fighting the war on terror. "

"But even the Navy has to let their people go home once in a while."

"I might get back there someday. Maybe when all the bad guys are dead."

"Where is *there*, David?"

"Southern California."

"And what about your family?"

"Mother, father, and two sisters. Last I heard they are all still in the San Diego area."

"You should call them."

"And tell them what, Anali? No, I do not want them worrying about me. Did you call your mother and tell her you were going after a terrorist?"

"Well, no, but…"

"We should go check in with the Prime Minister's security people, don't you think?" he broke in before she had time to finish her answer. She stood up and lifted her bag to her right shoulder.

"Are you coming with me this time, David?"

"Sure, but remember, I am your brother. They don't need to know otherwise."

They walked to the far end of the terminal and stopped in front of El Al's gate. Anali stopped and signaled to one of the Airline Security people before walking into the first metal detector.

The guard was dressed and carried himself like a soldier. He had a handgun holstered on his right hip and a standard Uzi slung over his shoulder.

"Step forward, miss," the twenty-something man said.

Anali opened her bag and reached inside, causing the guard to shift the Uzi until his hand found the trigger.

"I only want to show you my papers. I am with the government," she quickly explained, as she produced her identification.

"What is your business, Major," the guard asked.

"We would like you to take us out to the Prime Minister's plane."

"Wait here, Major," he said just before he turned and walked away.

When the guard returned, he explained that the Prime Minister was still at the University. I just spoke to one of his aides and he said they would be back around ten O'clock tonight. He asked that you wait, or come back in the morning."

"If you would, Cal," she said addressing the name tag over his heart," please call the Prime Minister's aide back and tell him or her, that Major Dupia just stopped by

92

to tell them that the Falcon is in town, and that he has a stinger missile; however, on second thought Cal, never mind. It's probably not important enough to bother with." She turned her back on the young soldier, leaving him standing there with his mouth open. Then she smiled and winked at David and said,

"Maybe we should just go shopping or sightseeing, brother."

"Let's go, sis. I have always wanted to see the pyramids," he said, following her away from the gate.

"Where to, David Stone," she asked just before starting the engine.

"Back to Cairo, driver. We need a change of clothes, and after that we can just play it by ear."

"Maybe I'll take you to see the pyramids later.

Chapter 11

Ahmed found Al Zaabi's younger brother working at
a milling machine in the rear of a machine shop. The shop
was just two blocks from the Mosque of Muhammad Ali,
and they had walked right by the place on their way up
from the river.

Ali Hussan was not happy to hear that Infidels had
killed his older brother, but he seemed even more unhappy
when he learned that Ahmed could not deliver the fifty
thousand dollar prize that was promised for the weapon's
delivery.

In a back room, hidden under a green tarp was the
American-made weapon Ahmed was seeking, but Ali was
holding fast to his demands.

"It is not as if I can just go to the bank and get you
your money, Ali," Ahmed argued.

"Al Zaabi gave his life, now you ask me to give you
the weapon without compensation."

"The Israeli dog flies away in less than twenty-four
hours. We cannot let that happen. You must trust me."

Ali was silent for a few seconds before shaking his
head no.

"I am sorry, Ahmed, but I owe the man who brought
it here. I must ask that you call someone. What if you are
not successful? What do I tell them?"

Askari stood with his right hand resting on the
ornate handle of his ceremonial dagger, ready to move on
Ali if the situation required. He knew that one way or
another, that stinger was coming out from under the tarp. It
would do so with Ali's blessing, or with his blood.

Hamza and Ayham sat quietly listening and waiting
for the go-ahead to remove the crate from the shop.

"You have my word that your price will be met, Ali,"

Ahmed said in a last ditch effort to convince the young Hussan to trust him.

"I have no other choice, Ahmed, but to demand at least half the money now. I have that much invested already."

Without another moments hesitation, Ahmed snapped his fingers and Askari produced his readied three-eighty automatic from his robe, and the startled Ali Hussan found himself looking down the cold steel barrel.

"You leave me no choice, Ali. Hamza! Ayham! please help Ali carry the missile back to the boat," he ordered.

The tarp came off, revealing the original olive drab crate that the surface to air stinger came in. Each man grabbed a rope handle and lifted it off the floor like a coffin. Askari joined them, and they headed out the door. Ahmed stopped and gathered up three AK47's and slung them over one shoulder. Then he found a canvas bag, dumped the contents on the floor, and filled the bag half full of clips and ammunition. The negotiations had ended and the stinger was on its way down the cobblestone streets.

The sun was low in the cloud free western sky, and the shadows were long when Ahmed caught up with his comrades.

Askari had let go of the crate and moved to the front, clearing the way for the others. Ahmed followed close behind the crate, watching to make certain that no one followed them.

The edge of night was upon the surface of the Nile when they approached Ayham's waiting boat. The day was coming quickly to an end and the lights across the river were waking up.

They loaded the weapon in the bow and Ahmed ordered Ali to get on board.

"You will go with us Ali. That way you will not lose sight of your property."

He climbed aboard without argument. He knew he

had pushed Ahmed too far. And, like it or not, he was now on his way to jihad.

Ali watched as the dry land slipped from the bow and the blue water of the Nile surrounded the watercraft. The outboard came to life and the boat began to swing around. A sudden surge of power forced him back into a seat, and all signs of the Muslim quarter disappeared off the stern.

Ayham plotted a course across the wide Nile Delta to a secluded cove they had found on the way upriver. The key to the plot to assassinate the Prime Minister was getting close enough to Cairo International Airport to watch the airliners take flight. They had to find the old Church and Ali Hussan knew the way. With the American technology they now possessed, victory was within their grasp despite the setbacks.

Chapter 12

As nightfall blanketed the Giza Plateau northeast of Cairo, the great Pyramids captured the moonlight. It was 7:25 pm when Anali and David pulled into the parking lot of the Mena House Hotel.

She looked her best in her new blue and white dress and the comfortable black pumps on her feet. He looked more like a tourist after packing away his tan cargo pants, pullover navy blue shirt and tennis shoes. The off-the-rack light grey slacks, white shirt, and brown dress shoes worked just fine for him. They had driven the twenty-two miles after an hour and a half of shopping at a mall near the Airport.

Anali locked the doors on the Saab and they were walking toward the hotel's front entrance when she suddenly stopped when she noticed a white limousine.

"Look David, the Syrians are here." She snatched the Syrian flag off the front fender. "It is probably the Ambassador. The one your friend Rashad works for," she continued after dropping the flag and wiping her feet on it.

"I take it you don't like Syrians much."

"I don't like Syrians at all, David. They are behind over half the terrorist attacks around the world."

"Maybe we should pay the Ambassador a visit before we leave in the morning."

"Maybe we should, David."

The forty-acre complex had one of the largest swimming pools he or she had ever seen. It was round in shape, and at least one hundred feet across. Well groomed lawns, palm trees, and imported stone walkways bordered the crystal clear water, and everything was illuminated by well-positioned ground lighting.

The Falcon's Final Flight

The Hotel and Casino was a massive white limestone building, and the arched doorways and windows looked like they belonged in the Valley of the Kings.

Inside the lobby, they could hear the bells and whistles going off, indicating that the hundreds of slot machines in the adjoining Casino were busy.

David booked a room on the second floor and then followed Anali into the Casino. It was like walking out of the Middle East and into Monaco, or even Atlantic City. There were men from all around the world in expensive suits, and women who were adorned in designer dresses and diamond jewelry. The smell of cigar and cigarette smoke lingered heavy in the air, and containers of beer, wine or whiskey filled every hand. Only the staff and dealers dressed the part of Egyptians, and their chosen era was Cleopatra's 34 B.C.

Video Poker and slot machines lined the walls. The Black Jack tables, Roulette wheels and Punto Banco Parlors were almost filled to capacity. There were women serving drinks, and several café's that served food of a western flavor.

Anali hesitated in front of a row of slot machines and searched through her bag for her wallet.

"I think I am going to try my luck, David."

"Okay, I'll go to the bar. What would you like?"

"I don't know, just whatever you're having."

He walked across the marble floor, around the gaming tables, and leaned his arm against the padded armrest that lined the bar. From what he could tell, all the alcoholic beverages were imported; however, it was the Coors beer logo on the handle of a tap that caught his eye.

"Do you have Coors in bottles," he asked, hoping the bartender spoke English.

Without answering, the slight little man wearing an ornate gold and white Galabya and bright red Fez turned and opened a cooler and produced a twelve ounce bottle then asked,

"One?"

"No, two please."

The Egyptian slipped the same hand back into the cooler and came up with a twin for the first bottle.

"That will be seven dollars American."

David produced a Canadian ten spot from his wallet and waited for his change. He then retraced his steps back across the busy room to where Anali was holding her own against the one armed bandit.

He placed his left hand on her left shoulder to get her attention and handed her a cold bottle of beer with his right.

"Oh, thank you, David," she said, bringing the bottle to her lips. He watched her curl her nose, taste her lips with her tongue, and then smack her lips together.

"What is this?"

"Coors, Anali. It is an American beer," he said, before taking another drink of his own.

"I have never tried beer before. It has a bitter aftertaste."

"I can go get you something else, if you'd rather."

"Oh, no, David. I will drink it. It is cold and not all that bad actually."

He sat down on an empty stool next to her for a few minutes and watched her feed the slot machine. He could see that she was enjoying herself, and he could hear the excitement in her voice as she rooted for the three Pyramids or camels to line up.

Anali was down to just a hand full of tokens when a long legged, scantily clad woman walked up behind David.

"Can I get you another beer, Sir, Madam," she asked in English.

"How much," Anali, asked without taking her eyes off the spinning wheels.

"There's no charge, madam, when you are gambling," the Cleopatra impersonator replied.

"Then I would like two please," Anali responded, holding out the all but empty bottle with her free hand.

"One for me, thank you," David said dropping two

99

of the three dollars left over from the bar on her empty tray.

He waited until the bar girl returned before he got to his feet and excused himself.

"I think I'll walk around, Anali,"

"I will be right here, David."

He made his way slowly around through the Casino, watching the other gamblers work their strategies against the house. The Black Jack tables were five dollars minimum, and roulette wheels accepted a one-dollar bet. The big money was being laid down in the Punto Banco Parlors. It was when David attempted to get close to one to get an idea how the game was played that a man in an expensive black suit put his hand out to stop his advance.

"This is a secure area, friend."

It was then that David noticed the radio receiver in the man's ear and a white plastic coated wire running from his ear and disappearing beneath his collar.

"I just wanted to see how the game is played." The bodyguard pointed to another parlor, and suggested that David learn how to play over there.

"Who is so important that he requires protection?"

"His Excellency, the Ambassador," the bodyguard said pointing to a portly gentleman at the far end of the table.

"Are you Syrian," David asked.

The guard gave David a look of concern and stepped between him and the entrance.

"I only asked because I noticed the flag on the limo in the parking lot," David said before turning and walking away.

He returned to where he had left Anali, and for another hour and twenty minutes, he watched her feed the one armed bandits and nurse her two free drinks.

It was 9:15, the machine had gone cold, and she had finally had enough. Enough of the gambling, and more than enough to drink.

They walked to an escalator and followed the signs to a fine restaurant on the second floor. He ordered another beer to drink with his prime rib and baked potato, and convinced a tipsy Anali to try the coffee.

"You were right, Anali. The Syrian Ambassador is here."

"Where?"

"Playing Punto Banco downstairs." She leaned forward and whispered,

"Do you have your little twenty-two with you?"

"No, I left it in the Saab, Anali."

"That's all right, David. I have my nine millimeter in my bag."

They spent an hour having dinner, and Anali pulled the handles on a few more slot machines on the way to the room. When they walked into the elevator, there was another man inside. Like the bodyguard at the parlor, he also had a transmitter in his left ear.

When the elevator stopped on the second floor and the door opened, David and Anali stepped out. David looked up at the level indicator above the door, and when the elevator stopped again, it was on the penthouse level.

I know where you live, Ambassador, David thought to himself.

It was a quarter to eleven when he opened the door to the suite and turned on the light. Anali turned left into the bathroom and David went across the room to the window and opened the drapes. The moon was high in the sky and cast a bluish light on the desert floor and, in the distance, the peak of one of the Great Pyramids marked the skyline.

He was enjoying the view, and giving some thought to the slimy son-of-a-bitch overhead in the Penthouse when he heard Anali's voice behind him.

"What time are you setting the alarm clock for, David?"

"I don't know. Seven or eight. What do you think?"

"Set it for seven. I promised to show you the Pyramids in the morning, and we need to find that Church before six tomorrow evening."

"Okay, Anali. Why don't you set the clock while I shower? Nice robe, by the way," he said as he walked past her.

The hotel had a theme, and the gold Cleopatra era robe was in keeping with that premise. It came very close to matching the drapes he had opened a few minutes earlier, and was two, maybe three sizes too big for her.

He showered, letting the warm water run for close to ten minutes. Then he shaved, using a razor that was compliments of the house, and opened the door and walked out into the bedroom.

Anali was already in bed, lying flat on her back under the covers looking up at the ceiling. A single lamp was the only source of light in the room and it was on what would be his side of the king size bed.

"Did you set the clock?"

"Yes. For seven."

The room went dark when he turned off the lamp. He dropped the matching robe and slid in under the light covers.

"I think I will sleep tonight, David. The beer you gave me made me tired."

"I gave you one. You ordered the last two."

"I know, and each one tasted better than the one before."

"That's what Coors beer does, Anali; it grows on you."

"It makes the room spin when you lie down and close your eyes." She turned over on her right side, and within minutes was out like a light.

David closed his eyes, but he could not get Abdul Salam al-Walid off his mind. He told himself that the man up in the Penthouse needed to be held accountable for ordering and paying for the assassination attempt on the Prime Minister, but how and when?

We could follow him in the morning and take him out somewhere between here and the University, or we could wait until after the Falcon has been dealt with and hope the son-of-a-bitch shows up in Alexandria at the compound. Or I could go upstairs tonight while Anali sleeps off her beer buzz, he thought to himself. And so, in the darkness of the hotel room, while lying there looking out through the French doors at the moonlit sky, he began to run a series of game plans over and over in his mind. Then, after weighing the pros and cons of each, he sat up and slipped quietly out of bed. He dressed in the moonlight that still filtered in through the glass, and slipped out the door into the hallway.

He pushed the up button on the elevator, and waited impatiently for the car to return. Once inside and after the doors closed he pushed the button marked "P" for Penthouse. When the elevator stopped again and the doors separated, he found himself looking into eyes of the same bodyguard that had refused him entry into the Punto Banco Parlor earlier in the evening. This time the man had removed his nine millimeter from under his coat and from the look in his eyes, it was clear that he was not happy to see David. He pointed his weapon at him, held his left hand out, and said,

"This is a secure area. I suggest that you go back downstairs."

"Oh, hell I must have pushed the wrong button," David said, but instead of backing into the elevator, he took one step forward, prompting the bodyguard to extend his arm. The blue steel barrel of his weapon pressed against David's chest, but as his lips tried to form a threat, a right hand caught him totally off guard. The startled man pulled the trigger and the hammer on his nine millimeter dropped, but David's left thumb came between it and the firing pin. Another hard right snapped the Syrian's head back for a second time, and his gun hand could not withstand the leverage. The bones in his wrist snapped and he released his grip on his weapon. David pulled hard and threw him back inside the elevator. The guard went head first against the back of the elevator, and then went down hard at his attacker's feet. David pushed the button and the doors closed behind his back and spat,

"We had the same conversation downstairs, and I didn't like your tone then." The bodyguard looked up, his eyes signaling his disbelief, and the rest of his face reacted to the pain that had befallen him.

David slipped the nine millimeter behind his back into his waistband.

"Get up on your feet," he ordered, but the Syrian did not respond.

"I said get up!" he snapped. The beaten guard reached up and found the stainless steel handrail that surrounded three walls of the elevator, and slowly helped himself up to his feet.

"When you took this job did you ever think you might have to die trying to protect the Ambassador?" The man hesitated for a second and then answered,

"It is my duty."

With the speed of a rattlesnake, David struck out with the heal of his right hand. The bodyguard's head snapped back for a third, and final time. His body shivered, then his knees buckled, and David moved to one side and watched him melt to the floor. The cartilage in his nose shifted upward with David's help, piercing the front lobe of his brain. His death was painless because it was quick. David pushed the button to open the elevator doors, and this time when the doors opened there was no one there to greet him. He reached down with his left hand and grabbed a handful of the dead man's collar, dragging his body out of the elevator, and into the Penthouse.

The entry way opened up into a large sitting room. The fifty-inch television was on, but muted. A yellowish glow was emanating from a gas fireplace across the room to his left in front of the large circular couch. The walls looked to be polished white limestone, and large expensive Persian rugs adorned the marble floors. The ceiling was three stories above the floor, and the wall directly across from the elevator was all glass. Beyond the sitting area on the right side of the room an ornate, circular staircase of the same white polished stone led up to the Master Suite. Thirty feet above the floor, centered in the ceiling, a crystal chandelier cast its passive light on the room. As David made his way across the room, he removed the bodyguard's nine millimeter from his waistband, and then one by one he ascended the stairs.

The second floor looked out over a balcony, and through the pane glass he could see the Great Pyramids basking in the moonlight. The Master Suite was dimly lit and engulfed in silence. The bedspread and blanket had been turned down, but the king size bed was empty.

David moved quickly across the carpeted floor to the only other door he could see, and pushed it slowly open. The room was very warm and steam lingered in the air close to the ceiling. He could hear the sound of the hot tub's jets, and noticed the partially-bald, grey head of a man resting against the rim of the large spa.

He moved closer until he could see that the Ambassador's eyes were closed, and he had a smile on his cleanly shaved face. David moved even closer and sat down on the edge of the tub. Then, to get Abdul Salam Al-Walid's attention, he pulled the slide back on the nine millimeter, letting it slam shut.

The Ambassador immediately opened his eyes and sat up straight.

"What is this, who are you," he asked, all the while looking around the room.

He was the same portly little man in the thousand dollar suit that David had picked out at the card table earlier that night. Somehow, sitting naked in the steaming tub of soapy water, he looked even smaller, and a whole lot less important.

His arms, that were now out of the water and resting on the rim of the hot tub, were wrinkled with age, and flabby. The hair on his sagging chest was as grey as what little remained above his ears in a band around his head, and his skin was white as snow.

105

"How did you get in here," he asked, still looking in vain for help.

"The same way you did, Abdul."

"What do you want?"

"I want the man who ordered the hit on the Israeli Prime Minister."

"What? I do not know what you are talking about."

David pointed the barrel down just above the surface of the water, about where the Ambassador's legs would be.

"Wait, wait, wait. Please don't shoot."

"Don't lie to me then, Abdul. I know that you sent a briefcase with a million dollars to your caretaker in Alexandria. I know that you ordered him to give the money to Ahmed when he arrived, and I know why the Falcon came to Egypt. So all I want from you is the names of the other people involved."

"Listen, mister, is it not obvious that an Arab state would want Omar Olmert out of the way?"

"So this was a government operation?"

"Of course it was."

"Why? You're in the middle of the Peace Talks."

"Are you Israeli?"

"No, Abdul, I am not Israeli."

"American?"

"That's correct."

"Then you would not understand."

"Try me."

"There will never be peace in the Middle East. The Israeli's do not want peace, and the Arab world certainly does not. As long as there is one Jew and one Arab, there will be conflict."

"Then why bother to even have the Peace Talks?"

"Because the rest of the world can not accept what I just told you."

David rolled up his sleeves and without any hesitation, reached down through the hot soapy water and grabbed Abdul by one ankle. As he pulled the one leg up, and Abdul's upper body went down, he placed his free hand on the Ambassador's chest and pushed him down into the steaming tub. Abdul struggled feverishly, but his head never found the surface. He grabbed David's arm and squeezed and his free leg tried to find traction on the slick bottom of the tub, but time ran out and his body was forced to breathe out. His legs stopped thrashing and his hand slowly relaxed.

"Now, Abdul, you won't have to attend anymore phony Peace Talks."

After a quick once over to dry his arms with a towel that he found folded neatly on the top of the vanity, David walked out of the bathroom and headed for the stairs.

He moved quickly down into the main room and made his way back to the elevator. He grabbed the dead bodyguard by his pant legs and dragged his body out of the foyer to the floor in front of the couch.

He had turned and was about to leave when he noticed that the elevator doors had closed and it was on its way down to the lobby. *There's always a stairway in the event of a fire,* he thought to himself. But then he noticed that the elevator was on its way back up, and it had just gone by the second floor; and then he remembered there was another bodyguard.

Damn, I'm getting sloppy; I almost forgot about the one that was in the elevator when we came upstairs.

He moved back to the elevator and stood just off to one side, waiting for the door to open. When the doors opened and the second of Abdul's protectors walked out into the foyer, David hit him on the side of his head with the nine millimeter he had taken off the first bodyguard. The man went down. His knees hit first and then he caught himself with his arms and started quickly back up. David applied a choke hold from behind as the man came up. The bodyguard pushed back slamming David into a wall, but failed to shake him loose. David applied more pressure as he was forced back against the wall again. Then, giving in to the lack of oxygen and blood supply to

his brain, the bodyguard slowly began to relax. He
released his grip on David's forearm and attempted to
strike him, but there was very little power behind the blow.
David could feel the man's body surrendering to the
pressure of the choke hold. He continued to apply
pressure until he was sure the man was finished, then he
stepped back, pulling the guard down to the floor from
behind, breaking his neck. David released his hold and
got to his feet, then dragged the second bodyguard into
the Penthouse and laid him out on the floor beside his
partner. He returned to the elevator and pushed the button
for the second floor.

Chapter 13

Four hours had passed when he opened his eyes and looked at the clock. Anali was no longer on the far side of the king size bed. He could feel her warm body pressed tight against his back, and she had laid her right arm across his side, and her hand was resting peacefully on his chest. He could hear that her breathing was steady, and he knew she was still fast asleep. He closed his eyes and tried his best to ignore the soft, naked flesh pressed against him.

The moon had departed from the sky, but the desert sun had not yet breached the Sudan. The room was cast into complete darkness and David was still awake.

Anali eventually stirred and said,

"David, are you awake?"

"Oh yes, I am very much awake."

"Can I ask you to do something for me?"

"Sure, Anali, what is it?"

"If things go bad tomorrow would you make sure my body gets home? I don't want to be buried in this place."

"I promise, Anali. If that should happen, I'll see that you get back to Tel Aviv."

"No, David, I want to go home to Montreal."

"Anali, the only thing that's going to happen tomorrow is that you and I are going to put an end to the Falcon's reign of terror."

"Promise me, David, that you will tell them to ship me home," she insisted, sounding as though she were about to cry.

"I promise, Anali."

She kissed him between his shoulders at the base

of his neck and said softly,

"Thank you, David."

He turned over until they were face to face and found her lips in the darkness, and then they did what had been on his mind from the moment he awoke and felt her bare breasts pressed against his back.

They embraced each other for a while and then made love a second time. It was five O'clock when David sat up on the side of the bed, and said,

"The sun is coming up. Maybe we should go down to the Casino and have breakfast. "

Anali sat up in the bed behind him and put her arms around his neck,

"Or you could lie back down and just hold me until seven O'clock," she purred.

He pushed back against her and lay back in the bed, took her in his arms and kissed her. They were both young, well conditioned, had been alone for a long time, and faced an uncertain tomorrow. They embraced and coupled for a third time before six O'clock and then, after fifteen minutes, she rolled out of bed and disappeared into the bathroom. He got out of bed and followed her. They showered together and then got dressed. The alarm had not yet sounded off and they were out the door, on their way to the elevator.

They stopped by one of the café's inside the Casino and had breakfast before walking up onto the Giza Plateau. David had seen pictures of the pyramids and had always mistakenly thought they were located in a remote desert area. Anali explained that in ancient times, that was in fact the case, but now urban development had reached out and surrounded the antiquities' site.

"Do you see that big Pyramid, David? That is the Pyramid of Khufu. It is referred to as the Great Pyramid. They were all built during the Fourth Dynasty, but Khufu is the oldest. The somewhat smaller one behind Khufu is the Pyramid of Khafa. He was Khufu's eldest son. The smaller one is Mykerinos, and the little ones are known as the Queen's Pyramids. Oh, and over there to the east is the Great Sphinx."

"When was the Fourth Dynasty?"

"2560 B.C."

"You do know your history."

"I should. I have three years invested in ancient history."

She took his hand in hers and they walked for close to an hour, following the path around the Ancient Egyptian Necropolis.

"We should be getting back. We still have a bad guy to find."

"I wish we had more time, David. Maybe we should come back after we do what we came here to do."

"That would be nice."

They made their way down off the Giza Plateau to the parking area in front of the hotel. David looked at his watch and then at the white limousine still parked where it had been when they arrived. It was 9:45 am. The last day of the Peace Talks was under way, and he knew that any minute someone was going to discover the mess he had left in the penthouse.

The drive back to the Airport was quiet, and it was not until they turned onto the road that would take them north of Cairo International Airport that the silence was broken.

"Anali, would you do something for me if I asked you to?"

"Yes, David. Anything."

"I would like it if you didn't go into the Church with me."

"Oh no you don't, David Stone. We have a deal, and nothing has changed."

"For me it has."

"Well, don't ask me to do that. I have waited four years for this day. I can handle myself as well as any man."

"Damn it, Anali, I know that you can handle

111

yourself, but someone needs to stay on the outside just in case any of them make a run for it."

"Nice try, but I am not buying, David. We do this together. Drop it, all right?"

He reached out and touched her cheek with the back of his fingers. "If you get yourself killed, Anali Dupia, I'll never forgive myself."

"Same back at you, David, but I am still going in with you."

Commercial buildings and warehouses surrounded the north end of Cairo International, and as far as the eye could see, there were houses. Some were newer residential subdivisions in, around, and close to the airport, but as they drove closer to the river, the houses were older, smaller, and even more congested.

They had driven back and forth between the river and the desert on roads just wide enough for one vehicle for close to an hour. They knew that there had to be an old Church somewhere close to the airport but so far, it had eluded them.

When Anali turned around at the end of a dead end road, she noticed a woman walking out of one of the small houses up ahead.

"When all else fails, ask for directions," she said and then pulled over to the side of the road.

The small older woman seemed reluctant at first, and turned around and started walking back toward her house. The woman stopped when she heard the woman in western clothes speaking in Arabic.

"I am trying locate an old Catholic Church."

The Egyptian woman looked at Anali for a full ten seconds before responding.

"There was an old abandoned Church not far in that direction." The woman turned and pointed west toward the desert and then continued,

"If you turn at the end of this road and go back south about three miles, you will see it."

Anali thanked her and turned to walk back to the

Ivan Wikert

Saab.
"There are no Christians there anymore," the old woman added.
"That's all right, ma'am. We're just out sightseeing," Anali answered.
She turned the Saab around in the middle of the road and headed in the direction the woman had pointed.
At the end of the road was the open desert, and for the next three miles they skirted the sand.
The old house of worship had withstood the centuries of persecution, but looked as if it was finally giving in to the encroaching wind and sand of the Sahara. The cross still stood atop the three stories of limestone and mortar, and cast a shadow that stretched out from the rooftop and marked the desert floor.
Built in the time of the Crusades, the Church and out buildings were surrounded by tall walls of stone. There was but one way in, and the gate was too narrow to accommodate even the Saab's narrow track.
Marked with ripples by the wind, the Sahara's sand had spread a yellowish-brown blanket across the courtyard, and drifts leaned against the outer walls. It was Anali that first noticed the fresh tracks in the sand. They started where the pavement ended, went through the gate, and marked the sand all the way to the Church's front door. It was evident from the direction of the tracks that four, maybe five people had walked in and, as yet, none had walked out.
"Do you think we could be that lucky," Anali asked as she removed her weapon from her bag and pulled back on the slide.
"I'll let you know how lucky when it's all over," David said in response as he opened the passenger side door.
Anali touched his arm,
"Wait, David," she said in a soft voice.
"What is it?"
"Do you remember back at the University when I asked you what you will do after this, and you said you

113

would give *after this* some thought?"

"Yes, I remember."

"So, David, what happens after this is over?"

"Well, Anali, if the Falcon is here, and he dies, then so does David Dupia."

"But what about David Stone?

"David Stone was never here. You know that. Now enough about *after this*, Anali Dupia. Let's go kill us a terrorist, and then we can talk about *after*." He slipped out of the car and they walked together through the gate into the courtyard.

The windows of the old Church had long ago shed their panes of stained glass, and the darkness from inside stared back out into the bright sunlight. The front door stood open and the same darkness filled the void.

"Why don't you wait here and cover me," David asked.

"You're a better shot, David; you should cover me." David had to move quickly to catch up to her, and they were kicking up sand as they ran full out for the front door.

They had all but closed the distance when a man dressed in brown cargo pants and a white shirt appeared in the open doorway. Ayham's eyes widened when he noticed the intruders running straight at him. He yelled, and instinctively raised his AK47. He had time to level it, but hesitated a split second too long, and David's twenty-two automatic sounded off once, and then a second time. Both rounds found their mark, high and close to the heart. Ayham was in shock but still on his feet when David made contact. His left hand found the barrel of Ayham's assault rifle, pushing it aside, and then without hesitation he put the cold blue steel of his service knife to Ayham's throat. The blade went in deep, cutting his throat from ear to ear and the Egyptian fell as if his leg bones had dissolved, landing hard on the dust covered floor.

Anali scanned the room, looking over the iron sights of her nine millimeter, then fired off two quick shots at a pair of fleeing legs near the top of a flight of stairs.

Someone cried out and then the sound of rapid gunfire quickly filled the room. The ceiling above their heads began to rain splinters, dust and lead.

David went to the right and Anali went to the left, ducking under one of the old wooden pews. He looked at her to make sure that she was safely tucked away, and she looked back at him, making a circle with her thumb and index finger to signal that she was.

The bullets continued to poke holes in the overhead for several minutes, and then, as quickly as it started, the gunfire stopped. A high pitched, loud Arab voice filled the silence from above.

"I am Ahmed Ali Muhammad, and I curse your souls, Infidels." Then the gunfire erupted again.

When the guns went silent for a second time, David looked back at Anali and winked,

"I am David, you Muslim dog. I have been dispatched from the Kingdom of Heaven to see that you never see paradise, he yelled."

There was a commotion from up above when Ahmed ordered Askari and Hamza to take the stinger up into the tower.

Anali stood up slowly, keeping her eyes trained on the old wooden staircase. David came out from under the pew that he had used as a shield, and walked to the center isle that faced the dust covered altar.

The sunlight coming in through the many open windows on the second level found the bullet holes in the floor above their heads and highlighted the smoke and dust that still lingered in the air.

Anali listened quietly and followed the sound of heavy footsteps over her head with her nine millimeter, and when the sole of a shoe blocked out the light she fired three rapid shots. Someone yelled out in pain and the old wooden ceiling began to splinter again.

Anali tucked and rolled when the first shot came through the floor, but she was not quite quick enough. One of the many armor-piercing rounds hit her in the calf of her leg. She did not cry out. She just went down and pulled herself across the floor to the left side of the stone altar.

David moved quickly between the pews and was headed to where she had fallen when, out of the corner of his eye, he noticed movement on the stairs. A soft-soled canvas boot appeared first, followed by a bloused white canvas covered leg. David flipped the switch turning on the laser sight, painted the exposed leg and fired. The man screamed out in pain, then disappeared from sight again above the stairs.

David backed over to where Anali was sitting next to the long abandoned altar and knelt down. She had already ripped the hem of her skirt and was tying off her wound.

"Let me have a look at that."

"I am all right, David. Go and finish what we came here to do."

"You stay down and out of sight, then Anali," he said, as he got back to his feet.

"Go on, David. I will be all right. It is a long way from my heart."

His rubber-soled sneakers made not a sound as he made his way to the staircase, but the first rung creaked beneath his weight. The smoke from gunfire was still heavy on the air and grew heavier as he neared the second level.

Another old stair tread squeaked and he thought to himself, *they have to know I'm coming up.*

One more step and his head would be visible to anyone on the second floor. He readied his weapon and took a deep breath, then popped up, quickly looking with haste for targets, but there were none to be found.

The room was long, but narrow; just like the one below without the furnishings. The smoke and dust still lingered in the air and was the only thing moving. There were two men, but neither posed a threat. One lay face down on the floor with blood spreading out from under his white Galabya. David figured that he was the one on the stairs that Anali shot when they first came in through the door. The second man was wearing a dark blue suit. He was sitting on the floor with his back against the wall across the room near the front of the building. His arms were hanging limp at his sides and, from the looks of it, most of his life had already spread out on the floor.

David noticed a ladder that ascended to the steeple. There were fresh, red blood stains on the rungs. He also noticed the open olive drab crate between himself and the injured man from Tyre.

He kept one eye on the ladder and the other on the downed terrorist, as he crossed the room, and stopped where he could see the inside of the crate. The stinger was not inside.

"What name do you want on your headstone, dead man," he asked in Arabic.

It was all the dying Askari could do to lift his head, and manage a gurgling cough that brought up blood, and a moan.

David turned and headed toward the ladder and looked up, then looked back at the dying man, and again in Arabic he said in a loud enough voice to be heard up in the bell tower,

"If you can fly, Falcon, you had better do it now because it's going to get very hot up there."

The problem was, David did not have a match or anything else that would start a fire.

Askari coughed again and then expired. His body slumped forward, and he slowly fell over onto his side.

David retrieved the AK47 that Askari no longer had any use for and returned to the three by three ladder well. He pointed the assault weapon straight up and pulled the trigger until the twenty round clip emptied itself.

"Last chance, Ahmed. You come down, or the fire comes up."

The words had hardly left his mouth when a voice from the top of the ladder said,

117

"I am coming down."

Another assault rifle like the one he had just emptied came crashing to the floor, followed by a nine-inch dagger with an ivory handle.

David used his foot to quickly pull the weapons from the base of the ladder and threw them out of the nearest window. He looked up and noticed that the man coming down the ladder was having a hard time. His right leg was of no use to him anymore, and tiny drops of blood were preceding his one-legged descent.

The big Sudanese filled the opening and his head was still above the door jam. He raised his long arms and turned around slowly before stepping out into the open room.

Hamza was wearing white canvas pants and a long shirt open in the front. The belt that belonged around his waist was tied around his right leg just above the knee to slow the blood flow. He looked down at David and said,

"The one behind you is Ahmed. He is the one they call the Falcon."

"It's funny just how much a man can change in just three days. I know what the slimy dog looks like, and that is not him. Nice try though," David said, just as he raised his weapon.

"Why don't you come down and join us, Ahmed?" David said in a very loud voice.

There was no answer verbally, just another ten round burst from an assault rifle. This time the armor piercing rounds came through the ceiling very close to where David was standing.

Hamza lunged forward, taking one round from David's twenty-two automatic in the stomach. The big man grabbed David with both hands firmly around his neck, picked him up over his head, and threw him across the room. He landed hard on his back and slid up against the crate, pushing the coffin-sized box three feet. Hamza made a growling sound as he closed the distance and reached down to grab David again, but David kicked him hard to the groin to slow him down, and then followed up with a scissor kick, sweeping the big man off his feet.

The old wooden planks shook and almost gave way when his entire six foot six inch frame came crashing to the floor. David was up onto his feet, and was on his way to retrieve his weapon before Hamza had time to realize that he too was down. The big man raised himself from the floor and jumped, but this time he went head first out through the second story window.

David retrieved his weapon from the floor and quickly returned to the opening. Below him, Hamza had retrieved one of the discarded assault rifles, and had it trained on David's position.

The big Sudanese fired, just missing him as he moved out of the opening. Then he fired six more times before David turned back into the opening to take a shot. But the giant was gone.

David's thoughts went to Anali who was downstairs wounded with an armed terrorist on the loose. But before he had time to turn around he heard two shots from what sounded like her nine millimeter, then three louder shots from an AK47, and after just a short pause, one more single shot rang out.

Hamza had come up the front steps and had stopped in the doorway when he saw Anali standing across the room with her weapon trained on him. She had managed to get to her feet and was balancing on her one good leg. Her first shot hit the big man high on the breastbone four inches below his collarbone, pushing him back against the door frame Her second missed by just an inch to the right, chipping a good-sized chunk out of the sandstone wall.

Hamza raised his weapon with one hand and fired three shots. Anali ducked down and rolled left as the six-point-two millimeter rounds splintered the back of the pew where she had been standing. She came up again with both hands steadying her weapon. Hamza turned his AK 47 on her again, but when he pulled the trigger, nothing happened. His twenty round clip was empty. Wounded and helpless, the big man looked Anali in the eyes, and spat at her in defiance. She closed her left eye and let her right one line up the iron sights. The fifty-grain slug left the end of her barrel, and the big Sudanese's head snapped back, and he withered and fell into the doorway.

David made a run for the stairs just as Ahmed came down the ladder.

Ahmed yelled out,

"I will cut your heart out, Infidel!"

His dagger sliced through the air from right to left in an upward motion. David threw a block with his weapon, catching the deadly blade between the barrel and the trigger guard on the small caliber handgun, interrupting the long knife's path toward his head. He planted his right leg and delivered a crushing front kick to his attacker's midsection. Ahmed groaned and fell back into the wall behind him. The pain doubled him over and his free arm instinctively went to his solar plexes. He gasped to recover the wind he had lost, but he somehow maintained his grip on the dagger.

David moved in and Ahmed raised his knife, extending it out in front of him, only to see it fly from his hand when a roundhouse kick hyper-extended his elbow. The beaten terrorist grabbed his arm and cursed his attacker.

David caught Ahmed with a crushing blow to the side of the head that sent him to the floor on the landing next to the stairs. He stepped over him, and with one hand wrapped in the collar of his suit coat, began to drag the semi-conscious Falcon down the old wooden stairs.

Anali was still sitting with her leg straight out in front of her on the floor. The wound had opened up during her exchange with the Sudanese and was bleeding again. She was in pain, but managed a smile when she saw David.

"I brought you a gift, Anali," he said, just before turning loose of the coat and letting Ahmed's upper body fall to join the rest of him on the floor.

"She looked at the heap on the floor, and then raised her head, locking eyes with David.

"Is he dead," she asked.

David reached down with one arm and turned Ahmed over on his back, slapping him hard across the face.

"Open your eyes, you murdering dog."

Anali picked her weight up with her arms and sat up straight.

"He doesn't look very dangerous now."

"No, Anali, the Falcon has made his final flight."

"Why didn't you kill him, David?"

"I made you a promise, remember. He is all yours."

"Help me to my feet. I want to be standing when I kill that son of a dog."

David took the hand she held up and assisted her until she had her balance on her one good leg. He could tell she was almost too weak to stand.

Her makeshift bandage was soaked with blood, her hand was cold as ice, and he could tell that she was fighting hard not to go into shock."

She leaned against David, holding her nine millimeter in her right hand.

"I called the Major General, David. He said he would send help," she managed to say just before going limp in his arms.

He lowered her back down onto the floor and sat down next to her, holding her head in his lap. He leaned back against the wall by the old stone altar beside her and listened to the sound of choppers coming in from the south.

"I hear the birds coming, Anali. You're going to be all right," he said as he slipped to the side and laid her head down gently on her bag.

The sound of helicopters seemed distant at first, but grew louder with every second that passed. David gently stroked Anali's black hair off her forehead and

The Falcon's Final Flight

kissed her. Then he stood up with her nine millimeter and pointed it down at Ahmed. The terrorist looked up at him and spat. The sound of one single shot rang out.

Chapter 14

When Anali opened her eyes she expected to see David, but she was alone. She was no longer in Cairo on the floor next to the stone altar in the old abandoned Church. She was in a bed at the hospital. She did not know when or how she got there, and she had no idea how much time had passed. The only light in the room was filtering in under the door. She turned her head and looked out the window at the stars, then closed her eyes again.

"How are you feeling, Anali," she heard a woman ask.

"Where am I," she asked before fully opening her eyes.

"You're in the infirmary at Tel Nof Air Force Base, my dear." The nurse lifted Anali's right arm to inspect the connections between her IV and the monitors.

"Is David here," she asked.

"Who?"

"David. He was with me in the Church."

"I wouldn't know about that, Anali. All the Major General said was that I should take extra special care of you, and that I was to call him the minute you woke up."

"Is the Major General here?"

"I am sorry, he is not. He is in Tel Aviv."

"Where is my bag? If you would give me my cell phone...."

"I am sorry, Anali, the Army took everything."

"Would you call the Major General now, nurse?"

"I will just as soon as I finish checking your vitals. And my name is Janette."

"Janette, my vitals are just fine. I have to know what happened to David."

123

The Falcon's Final Flight

"I will be right back, and then you will have to let me do my job," Janette said sternly just before she turned and left the room.

It seemed like an eternity to Anali before Janette reappeared in the doorway. This time she was not alone. She had a very tall man in an Army uniform following her.

"Anali, this gentleman...."

The tall, sandy haired man with oak leaves on his shoulders interrupted Janette before she had time to say his name.

Anali, I am Major Amnon. I will try to answer all your questions. Please close the door on your way out, nurse."

"But I need to...."

"No, nurse, you need to do as I say, please." His steel-eyed stare made it clear that he meant it.

Janette turned on her heel, and this time stormed out into the hallway. The man who had just introduced himself as Major Amnon walked slowly across the room to the window, picked up the only chair in the room with one very large hand, and carried it back over to her bedside.

"Before we get to your questions, Anali, I want to tell you that all of Israel is in your debt. I have already heard from very high up that you will most definitely receive the Aleh-State Warriors Order for your service to the country. So, that said, what is it you would like to know?"

"Where is David?"

"Who?"

"David Stone. He was with me at the old Church."

"There was no one with you, my dear."

"Yes there was, damn it. And I am not your dear!"

"All right, Anali, let me put it to you another way. There is no David Stone. There never was a David Stone, and this is the last time you will speak his name. The Prime Minster's staff are, as we speak, drafting your statement. You acted alone. You just happened to run into the Falcon just outside Hebron. You walked up beside his car and shot him." Then the Major put his index finger to his own head in the middle of his forehead, and continued. "Right about here. End of story."

"Fine. I do not care what story you want to tell, Major Amnon. However, here in this room, with the door closed I want you to tell me where David is. If you do not tell me, I will go to the press with my own version of the truth."

"No you won't, Major Dupia. Soldiers follow orders."

"I will resign."

"All right, Anali. I told you the truth. There was no one with you when the extraction team picked you up. I can show you the reports from the boots on the ground."

"But David Stone was there, Major. It was he who killed the Falcon, not I. So, cut the crap and tell me where he is."

"I don't know where David Stone is, Anali."

"But you know him don't you? And do not lie to me; he told me about you. You're the one who drove him to the beach."

Major Amnon hesitated for a second or two and then said,

"There is an organization that is part of our government that...how can I put it? Is so deep undercover that even the Mossad is unaware of its existence. The organization's mandate is to train operatives to terminate people who are enemies of the state. The first time I laid eyes on David Stone was three months ago when he walked up to the gate at the training camp. He said he was a United States Navy Seal, and that he came to volunteer."

"Wait just a minute, Major. You said that no one else knew about the program."

"I guess I was mistaken, because David knew all about it."

"How is that possible?"

"I figured that it was because the American's have

125

eyes and ears everywhere."

"But you must have checked out his story, Major Amnon. "

"No, Anali I did not. I just took him at his word. I welcomed him to our little family, no questions asked."

"Someone, somewhere has to know where he is."

"Major Dupia, I have trained a whole lot of men for many different operations, but none ever impressed me the way that American did. He had not been in camp three days before I knew he was the one, and in two short weeks, the entire staff agreed with me. So I trained the American who called himself David Stone to go into Tyre, find the Falcon, and kill him. The last time I saw David, he was walking into the Mediterranean. That was five days ago."

"Maybe he went back to the training camp," she suggested as a possibility.

"Not likely; we closed it down the day the operation started. My guess is that he has gone back to his ship."

Then Major Amnon raised his hand to his lips, placed his index finger against them, and shook his head slowly from side to side.

"Now can we agree not to speak of him again, Anali? There was no American involvement. Do you Understand?"

She glared up at him from her bed as he stood up, but said nothing.

"Do you have any other questions?"

"No."

"Excellent. In four hours, a helicopter will be here to transport you to Tel Aviv. I have given the nurse back your clothes and your bag. I had them washed and dried for you, so I would appreciate it very much if you would be ready to go. Oh, and Major Dupia, when I leave this room you will forget that we had this conversation."

Major Amnon's shadow had not yet removed itself from the tile floor before Anali had swung her legs off the side of the bed and she was sitting up. She pushed the button to summon Janette, and while she waited for her to return, her mind went back to the warm morning on the fifteenth.

"Aren't you coming with me," she remembered asking.

"No, Anali, I am not really here, remember," was his answer.

She had tears in her eyes when Janette came in through the door.

"What is wrong, Anali?"

"Oh, someone I love has gone away and I never got the chance to say goodbye."

"I am sorry to hear that. Is there anything I can do?"

"No, Janette, but I will find him, with or without the Army's help."

"I brought you your things, Anali." All of her clothes had been washed, and after a quick look inside she determined that everything seemed to be in her bag. She dressed for the chopper ride back to Tel Aviv, and let Janette push her wheelchair to the elevator. Janette had stayed with her while she ate breakfast, and they shared a pot of tea until it was time to go. Janette pushed her wheelchair all the way to the heliport.

"Take care of yourself, Anali, and I pray that you will find him," she said as she hugged her, and handed her the crutches.

Anali said goodbye to Janette and accepted the help of two young airmen to get up inside the bird. The blades began to pick up speed and made a popping sound as they gathered the cool morning air. The chopper lifted slowly off the ground above the tarmac, hovering briefly, and then it was up, up, and away. The gunship climbed above the Promised Land and found the desert sun hiding behind the horizon. The shadow of the chopper hurried by over the fields and settlements below, and far off in the direction they were flying she could see the blue water of the Mediterranean. In less than a half hour, the helicopter had made the crossing between Tel Nof Airbase and was hovering over a heliport at Tel Aviv International Airport. The bird slowly descended from above the rooftops and gently touched down.

Anali noticed a dark sedan parked nearby and a tall slender man leaning against the passenger side door. His right hand was on his head holding his hat in place against the force of the wind coming off the blades, and his left was resting on the arm of a wheelchair.

When the young airman opened the door, Anali could see that it was the Major General's driver, Sid Westbrook. When he noticed her moving toward the open door, he ducked his head and started pushing the chair toward the chopper.

The blades were still turning overhead, and the engine had not yet fully quieted down when she stepped down onto the ground.

"Welcome home, Anali!" He yelled to be heard over the whining engine.

"Thank you, Sid. Is the Major General in the car?"

"No, Major, he is not. I am to deliver you to his residence."

She handed her crutches to Sid, turned her back to him and sat down in the chair, took control of the wheels herself, and headed for the sedan under her own power.

He walked ahead of her and opened the door to the back seat. Anali rolled up beside the front passenger side door and reached for the handle,

"If you don't mind, Sid, I think I'll sit in the front."

"Oh no, Major, you can sit anywhere you like."

She stood up, using the door handle as a prop. Sid folded the wheelchair and put it away in the trunk, and then slid behind the wheel. In less than ten minutes, the dark sedan was skirting the coastline and was now moving south along the waterfront.

It was a calm, clear morning, with a welcome coolness in the air, compliments of the incoming sea breeze. In the early morning, through the haze that lingered across the surface of the blue Mediterranean, the ever-present American gray ships lined the horizon, and shopkeepers along the waterfront were just starting to open their doors.

Sid stayed to the left following R. Herbert Samuel Parkway, and stopped in front of a line of condominiums.

"We're here, Major. Give me just a minute to get your chair."

"I will try the crutches, Sid. It isn't that far."

"Alright, Major. You go on ahead. I'll bring it along just in case."

Anali had no trouble negotiating the three concrete steps leading up to Sol Kline's front door. She rang the bell and pushed the ornate oak door open, not waiting for a response from inside,

"It is me, Anali," she shouted.

The Major General was sitting in an overstuffed brown leather recliner in his living room. He had been watching through the picture window, and was aware that his sedan had pulled up out front.

"In here, my dear," she heard him respond.

She followed the sound of his voice and stopped in the doorway.

"Come in and sit down, Anali. We have a lot to talk about." She moved to a chair, leaned her crutches against the arm of the chair and sat down.

"How are you, my dear?"

"I am all right, Sir. Or at least I will be when my leg heals."

"The Prime Minister called me. He expressed that he would like to meet you. He wants to tell you in person how proud he is of you."

"Sir, I didn't do all that much, but the Prime Minister owes his life to David Stone."

"What happened out there, Anali?"

She started at the point where the Falcon walked out through the gate at Port Alexandria, and explained everything that happened, leaving out only the personal parts. She explained about the Egyptian driver Rashad Attar, and the Syrian Ambassador, Abdul Salam al-Walid who had put up the funds to have the Prime Minister assassinated.

"Ambassador Walid should be put on the list of bad guys," she suggested.

Hearing what she had just said, Sol Kline leaned back in his chair.

"I would put Al-Walid on the list Anali, but the man is dead."

"What?"

"Ambassador Abdul Salam Al-Walid is dead."

"How?"

"The old vulture drowned in his bathtub."

"Where?"

"In the Penthouse at the Mena House Hotel."

"When?"

"His driver found him the morning of the sixteenth."

"We were there, Sir. We stayed there on the fifteenth."

"I know that, Anali."

"Well, Sir, it could not have happened to a nicer guy. What are they saying? Did he have a heart attack?"

"I doubt that."

"Why is that?"

"Well, they found both his bodyguards. They are still waiting on the Medical Examiner's report, but they are reporting that one of the guards neck had been broken.

Anali leaned back in her chair and a smile came to her lips.

"David," she whispered. Then she continued with her story.

"I remember David dropped the son-of-a-dog on the floor and then he helped me get to my feet, but then everything went black."

"Anali, the report I received from the commander of the extraction team doesn't mention David. When they arrived on the scene, they found you unconscious on the ground floor. There were five terrorists, all of them dead. Three downstairs and two upstairs. They found the stinger in the bell tower. I will let you read the report, Anali. There is no mention of David anywhere in it."

"Did they mention my Saab in the report?"

"No, they did not." She smiled again.

"Well, Major General, I know now how David left the Church."

"There's just no way of knowing that for certain Major. They just might not have noticed your car."

"Sir, do you think David Stone left because he was afraid the soldiers coming in on the choppers might arrest him?"

"Arrest him for what, Anali?"

"I do not know. I am just trying to figure out why he left."

"My dear, I don't think that young man feared anything, or anybody. I remember asking him what he would do if he were me, and after I explained that I could not blow the Sea Eagle out of the water as he suggested, he answered.

"Then just get me on that boat. No, my dear that young man did not leave out of fear."

"Major General, I do not want any medals, and I don't want to meet with the Prime Minister. I just want you to find David before the Egyptians do."

"Who said anything about medals?"

"Oh, some Army Major, named Amnon."

"Really? You are the second person who brought up that name."

Sol Kline looked into her face and saw the resolve that went along with her words.

"I'll have the team watch for one of the credit cards to surface, and if he uses the passport we gave him we will find him."

"What about the United States Navy?"

"I will see what I can do, Anali. Until then, I want you to get some rest. Sid will drive you to one of our apartments on the base, or if you would rather, to a hotel. You should take some time to heal and collect yourself."

"All right, Major General, but you and this entire country owe me, so find David," she said as she got back to her feet.

"I still have my cell phone, so call me when you find him. I will be at a hotel," she continued as she negotiated the crutches toward the door.

"Good day, Anali," he said as she walked way.

Her meeting with Sol Kline had lasted only forty minutes, and the ride to a hotel near the waterfront less than that. Sid removed the wheelchair from the trunk, and handed her her bag when she sat down. She said goodbye to him at the car and pushed her way to the lobby on her own.

"I would like a room overlooking the water," she said to the clerk.

"For just yourself, ma'am?"

"It is Major Dupia, and I would like the room for the week," she said as she handed him her credit card.

The slender little man swiped the plastic through his machine and handed it back to her. He then directed her to a hallway explaining that the room was on the first floor but it had an unobstructed view of the marina and the Mediterranean.

"I thought that because of the wheelchair you would prefer being close to the café."

She thanked him before turning and heading for the hallway, but stopped when she found herself in front of the café he had just mentioned. The aroma from the kitchen filled her nostrils, and she realized that she was hungry.

She ordered the Israeli salad, cucumbers and tomatoes on a bed of lettuce, and sat alone while she ate, watching the white sails of pleasure boats move across the blue water.

The room was nice. Not overly large, but with the drapes pulled back it had a nice open view of the Mediterranean. She showered, letting the hot water sooth the ache in her leg, and for the first time inspected her wound.

The bullet had entered through the back of her leg half way between the knee and the ankle, requiring only three stitches. The dull pain that she still felt was from where the six point two caliber bullet had chipped the bone on its way through her leg. The exit wound was larger, and there were nine stitches which formed an almost perfect X.

She closed the drapes and dropped the towel on the floor, turned down the bed and, without bothering to dress, crawled between the sheets. It was not long before her dreams carried her back to Cairo, and into David's waiting arms.

The sun had not yet found the horizon, and light still gathered behind the drapes when Anali was awakened by the sound of her cell phone. She opened her eyes and waited for the fog to lift from her mind. Then she rolled over onto her back and stretched her arm out in search of the persistent ring.

"Hello," was all she offered up.

"Major Dupia, I don't know if you remember me. My name is Bayla Kann. I work for Major General Kline."

"Yes, yes! Did you locate David?"

"No, Major, but I was instructed to inform you of any movement regarding credit cards. Would you mind taking a quick look at the one you used when you checked in?"

"Why," Anali asked as she slid out of bed to retrieve her bag.

"Because someone used the Visa card that I had prepared for David Dupia at the same hotel where you are now."

Anali turned her bag upside down and shook the entire contents out onto the bed. She quickly found and opened her leather wallet that contained her identification and credit cards. Her hopes were dashed when she noticed the name David Dupia on one of two identical Visa cards. Then with Bayla hanging in silence on the phone, Anali searched even deeper.

133

The Falcon's Final Flight

She soon found out that tracking David Stone through credit card or passport use was no longer a possibility. Sometime after she had blacked out and before the choppers arrived at the old abandoned Church, David had slipped everything that had the name David Dupia on it into her leather wallet. Then something else he had said came to mind. All of a sudden, she felt flush and tears welled then spilled from her dark brown eyes. "When the Falcon dies, Anali, so does David Dupia."

"He is gone!" slipped from her quivering lips, and Bayla was left in silence once again.

It was only after two full minutes had passed that she managed to tell Bayla that both of the credit cards and passport that she had fabricated were lying on the bed in front of her. Then she said,

"Tell the Major General that I am leaving. I am going home to see my family, and I don't know if I will be coming back."

"Oh, he will be sorry to hear that, Major."

"Just tell him that when the Falcon died, so did Major Dupia."

She hung up the phone and placed a call to El Al. The next flight scheduled for Montreal was at 11:45 that night. She had two and a half hours to get dressed, call a cab, check out and get back across the city to the Airport.

At 11:45, as scheduled, El Al Flight 1121 taxied out from the terminal. Fifteen minutes later, the 747's wheels departed from Israeli soil. At the stroke of midnight, the Israeli government issued a state of high alert.

On the front pages of every newspaper were pictures of Ahmed Ali Mohammad, showing the notorious Falcon's body. The headlines varied slightly, but all made it clear that the terrorist was dead, and that one of Israel's Secret Police had killed him.

Within minutes, riots broke out in Southern Lebanon, Syria and the Gaza strip, and rockets were launched on nearby Israeli cities. Israeli tanks and bulldozers rolled into the West Bank and Gaza to protect

134

outlying Jewish settlements, and warplanes and gun ships took to the air over the entire Israeli state. As the news filtered over the plane's television and radio stations through the headphones and into the ears of the two hundred and thirty passengers on board, Anali sat quietly looking for stars from her window seat.

Four years, two months, and one week after the car bomb went off in the Holy City, she was going home.

The silver bird was high above the clouds, and through the thick glass the heavens seemed close at hand. Anali removed her headphones, turned off her overhead light and let sleep, and her dreams come drifting in.

The End

3627352

Made in the USA